CHASING CASEY

A BOOK OF FICTION
WRITTEN BY M. TAITANO

ALL RIGHTS RESERVED
NO PART OF THIS BOOK SHALL BE
REPRODUCED OR STORED IN RETRIEVAL
SYSTEMS OR TRANSMITTED BY ANY MEANS
WITHOUT PERMISSION FROM S. SIOBHAN

THIS BOOK IS A WORK OF FICTION
IT DOES NOT REFLECT THE EXPRESS
VIEWS AND OPINIONS OF
THE WATCHTOWER, BIBLE
AND TRACT SOCIETY

FIRST EDITION

ISBN: 13-978-1491238431
ISBN: 10-1491238437

COPYRIGHT © 2013
S. SIOBHAN

PRINTED IN U.SA. BY S. SIOBHAN

FROM THE AUTHOR

THANK YOU TO THE FOLLOWING FRIENDS AND FAMILY FOR THEIR HELP AND INPUT WITHOUT WHICH THIS BOOK WOULD NOT HAVE BEEN POSSIBLE

BUZZY BUZZARD	TED WALLY
JONATHON SWANSON	C. J. HAVENS
DAVID HECKMAN	C. KLATT
JERRY STALLINGS	JAMESBRETT
JESHUA ANDERSON	SGT. POE
WILL MARROQUIN	J. KNOWLES
MR. & MRS. THOMAS	DUNCAN DAVIS
MICHAEL EMERSON	HELEN TAYLOR
JACK CONSTANZA	CHRIS BRAZIL
THE SPRINGFIELDS	CLIFTON SMITH
RAYMOND & AUTUMN HARRIS	MITCH DAWSON

SPECIAL THANKS TO
SHEILA SIOBHAN – EDITOR

SUSIE ANDERSON-MEANS
RICHARD TAITANO
JEHOVAH GOD

DEDICATION

I started out this book with the purest intentions. Having lost custody of my daughter under circumstances irreversible, I found myself wanting to tell her my side of the story. Sure my story is everywhere. One need only look up my name on the computer and there for all to see is 'my story'. Well, America's Most Wanteds' version anyway. It does not tell who I truly am, nor would it tell the miraculous circumstances into which Angelica, my daughter, was born.

So pen met paper and off I went, writing my autobiography. I felt relieved somehow, knowing that finally she would truly know not only who her father was, but more importantly, who he became.

Then unexpectedly, in the midst of it all, her mother died, tragically, at the age of 32. She had lapsed into a coma after her injuries from a car accident finally caught up with her. A hole was left in my heart, magnified by the fact that Angelica was too young to truly know the facts of it all, but would have need of later.

Finally, I finished my autobiography. However, after reading it over, I realized it was a bit too graphic for a 13-year old. In fact, it was a bit too graphic even for me, well, the 'new' me. So how was I going to tell the story of her family? How would I explain a story that seems questionable at the least and outright unbelievable at most? How could I also teach her the lessons I had learned so long ago? And more importantly, how could I bring her to my God and Father?

So now, you have the makings, motives and settings for "Chasing Casey".

So, this is a book of fiction, dedicated to my daughter, Angelica. "Although at times it will feel like it, you are never truly alone my daughter".

LOVE, DAD

CHAPTER 1

SEATTLE RAIN

People say it always rains in Seattle, but it isn't true. Truth is, it only rains when they're planning on going out, Micah chuckled wryly to himself as the drizzle streamed across the windshield while he drove toward the old abandoned industrial area in Pioneer Square.

The tracking device he placed in her shoes the week before just might save her now, as his worst fears were realized, the news having broke earlier today of her kidnapping.

CNN was reporting that she was nowhere to be found, even though her father, the lawyer and aspiring politician, was spending vast amounts of money and human resources trying to locate her. They wouldn't find her though, Micah knew. But, thankfully, he could and hopefully would before it was too late.

Somewhere among these buildings a scared teen-aged girl has just had her life turned upside down by some rather ruthless men. He knew because originally he was the one that had trained them, had hired them.

They were indeed lawless, ruthless creatures of the night who loved nothing and no one. That is, except for money. Money was their god as it had been his once upon a time. But now he has changed. It was just too bad he couldn't convince them to do the same.

Micah contemplated all of this as he drew closer to the location indicated by the blinking red light on his cell phone. How close had he actually come to becoming just like them? Too close, if he were being honest with himself. He had long since grown out of the drastic mood swings that had plagued him as a youth, yet this current situation was a graphic reminder of the paradox he had been in. That of being both a genius and bipolar.

In those days when he had been on an upswing, swimming with the clouds, a good idea soon seemed like a GREAT idea that couldn't be swayed for the sheer force of its zealous creativity.

Still, when he was on a downswing and circling the drain, those very same ideas could plummet him beyond despair, speed past the depths of madness, take a hard right turn sideswiping reasonability while simultaneously spiraling to a stop just beneath the bowels of twisted logic. It was from such a world that the kidnapping plan had been born.

Sure, he would later abandon it unceremoniously in the emergency exit of his demented past. Yet here it appears again today like a reoccurring nightmare played out on the stage of a daytime talk show waiting for the DNA tests to reveal the plan to be his own.

They had to be stopped! That was for sure. But they wouldn't go quietly, no, he needed a better plan and wished he had more time. That's actually why he'd begun following her, their mark, just a few days prior.

He drove along thinking of that first day, hoping they wouldn't go through with it. Just five days ago, wasn't it? Yes. She was about seventeen and was quite possibly one of the most strikingly beautiful girls he'd ever seen.

Maybe that first moment was when he'd really begun to second guess this whole thing, he wasn't sure. But there she had been, innocently standing at that bus stop after school, completely unaware of the danger she was in. There was something about her that pulled him in. She was so vibrant, alive. But he felt creepy watching her like that, just like them across the street. "So obvious in that blue van, guys" he whispered, as he kept an eye, both on her and them.

But if that wasn't creepy enough, he felt doubly creepy sitting on her bed that night after he'd snuck in to place the tracking devices in her shoes. Somehow he'd cut himself climbing in through the window. He chided himself as he wrapped a towel around the fresh wound. "Probably the rose bush," he whispered.

It was a necessary risk though. He had no idea if they were going to go through with it or when they planned to do it, if they did.

As he'd looked around her room that day, seemingly so long ago, he'd tried to pick up on what kind of girl she was. Athletic from the soccer trophies, talented from the pink guitar in the corner, and somewhat spiritual from the Bible on the desk.

"Well, young lady, you're going to need all of that if we're going to get out of this mess," he said under his breath as he turned his truck into the abandoned lot.

Time to do an equipment check; it always seemed to calm his nerves at moments like these.

Adrenaline coursed through his veins, dilating his pupils and firing his heart to an almost audible rate. "OK ski mask, check, knife, check, utility tool (one never knows when it'll come in handy), check. Finally, the butterfly knife, check, check and check", he whispered to himself.

Dressed in black camouflage and ski mask, he cautiously exited the black Ford Ranger. Be careful Micah, he counseled himself, they could be anywhere near here. Routinely placing duct tape over the license plates, he took off running toward the darkened warehouse, as her red dot lit up his screen.

"She's somewhere in there", he muttered to himself. He calculated that she had been in their custody for about twenty hours. It wouldn't be long before the damage done to her would be permanent, if it wasn't already too late.

Approaching the window, it became immediately obvious that he would need a boost to get up there. Yet another disadvantage of being just five foot nine, he thought to himself while he doubled back onto the streets looking for and eventually finding an old milk crate that would serve his purpose.

"Oh!" he came crashing down from the window ledge, slamming his head on the concrete, having slipped off of the crate. "Dangit! Micah! Get ahold of yourself!"

He hadn't quite expected to really find her in the very first place he checked, so when he peered in and saw the red headed girl tied to the bed, well, he reasoned, it would've taken anyone by surprise. But it was definitely her. Four ropes held her hands and feet to the bed posts respectively.

He thought for a moment of how, originally, he himself was planning all of this (before his conversion of course). He had specifically trained the men NOT to keep her in a room with an outside window. This, in order to prevent an easy rescue, which he would now have to attempt. Hopefully, he thought to himself, they also didn't listen to my advice about placing silent alarms on the doors and windows either.

Foolish as they were however, he was under no delusions that they wouldn't rape or even kill her if given the right amount of time. Gotta go boy, he encouraged himself as he began to play with the window latch, hoping it would give in easily. Breaking the multi-tool on the window latch, the device finally gave way with a snapping sound.

He vaulted head first into the room. Getting his bearings, he looked up to find her yanking violently on her restraints as she prepared to defend herself from the clumsy intruder. "Listen, Casey is your name right?" She nodded. "I'm here to rescue you, but if we're going to get out of here alive I need you to be quiet as I take off the blindfold and gag, ok? Don't scream."

She jolted upright in the bed, immediately noticing the ski mask he was wearing, but calmed down as he began to cut away her restraints. She sat there quivering in her school uniform she had been wearing since the whole ordeal had begun days ago. She sat motionless for a few tense moments while her eyes adjusted to the darkness, glancing around until her attention finally rested on the open window. Noticing her focus, he whispered "the window is too high for us to just climb out, so we'll have to move this bed over to the window. I'll go first, then catch you as you come out after."

"But," she asked nervously, "what if they come in here after you've gone?" He looked around, found a high backed chair and shoved it under the door handle. She nodded, seemingly satisfied. She was strong for her age, he thought, as they moved the far too noisy bed to the window. "Hey! What's going on in there!" Someone yelled just as Micah exited the window. "Oooow!" Micah protested as Casey landed on top of him, having leapt out in a panic, knocking the wind out of him as she took off running.

"Wait!" he screamed. "This way! Trust me." She paused to look at the masked man sarcastically, as if to say '*really?*' A surrealistic moment that was short lived as the kidnappers began filing out of the building searching for them. Seeing them, she turned on a dime, convinced, and followed Micah to the waiting truck.

They drove along at speed, darting the glances of pedestrians who stared at the strange sight of the ski masked driver. Each time they passed an intersection or slowed for a red light she looked as though she were ready to jump out and break for freedom. Yet each time something kept her inside the vehicle. Maybe, he thought, he was gaining her trust.

"Who are you?" she asked, finally breaking the silence.

"Angel."

"*Really*? That's what you're going with?"

"Angel's a good name, what's wrong with Angel?"

"Nothing ….. if you're a *girl*."

"Well maybe I am a girl, you can't tell with this mask on."

"Please, you're no girl. Why are you wearing that thing anyway?"

"Maybe I don't want you blabbing to the reporters who I am."

"Well, who are you? One of the kidnappers with a change of heart?"

"No. Just a friend who thought you could've used some help."

"My *friends* don't wear ski masks."

"Well I do."

"Then you're not my friend."

"Oh boo hoo, then I guess I'll just take my mask off so that I can be your friend. NOT."

"You're not a kind person either."

"Well what exactly makes a friend? Who really is your neighbor?"

"Are you getting philosophical with me *mister* ski mask?"

"Angel."

"Are you getting philosophical with me *mister* ski mask Angel?"

"I should've just left you there."

"Why didn't you? In fact, how did you find me to begin with?" Silence once again filled the cab as they drove on while he was considering just how much information to give or not. It was true, she deserved an explanation, but the fact remained that eventually she would be interrogated and then possibly spill the beans on him, albeit unintentionally.

"Sorry bout that Angel. I guess I was just trying to keep things light."

"It's ok, you've been through a lot. Listen, you seem like a good person with a bright future. I hope

17

you don't turn into one of those people who, because of one traumatic event, decide to harden their hearts forever and then one day they find that they have become the very monster they once despised."

"You sound like you speak from experience."

"Maybe I do, but this isn't about me, it's about you continuing to be the fun loving person that everyone knows. Just try to live your life without fear, ok?"

"I don't know, maybe it is about you, you're the one wearing the ski mask."

"Will you get off the ski mask already?"

"Well, it's creeping me out. I should just yank the thing off."

"Don't. It's best for both of us if I remain anonymous."

"Anonymous? Well I don't know how anonymous you really are. For example, you know my name, you knew where to find me, and you think I would probably recognize you without the mask. So I do know you somehow already, right?"

"No", he responded with a bit too much bass in his voice.

"So if I don't know you personally then that means that the people I would've told your description to would've known you, right? So you must be one of my dad's friends from back in his military days."

"Will you just stop asking questions? You're not going to extrapolate my identity."

"Extrapolate. Hmmm, big word. So let's see, you went to college, military tactics, philosophical conceptions .... West Point! Right? You're probably a chaplain or something. Or no, a chaplain trained killer agent, yeah, that's good, a religious killer."

"Ok, now you need to shut up."

"Shut up!"

"Be quiet .... is that better?"

She nodded.

"Ok" he continued, "the police are going to ask you all kinds of questions, questions that you may or may not want to answer, but it's important that you are honest with them, with the exception of any info dealing with me."

"Why?"

"Because little miss nosey, those kidnappers are still out there and if I'm going to stop them from making another attempt on you then I need to be free to do that, a freedom that I will not have if I'm in an interrogation room for the next few hours while they get away."

"Navy Seal, huh? I get it, you're not officially here are you?" she asked.

"Here, take this" he said, ignoring her question while handing her the knife. She turned it over in her hands getting a feel for it as though she were an experienced weapons expert testing a new product. It was a butterfly knife specially made years ago for a different purpose entirely, but for now it would have to protect her, he thought.

"What am I going to do with *this*?" she asked incredulously.

"Protect yourself if the kidnappers come back, although I doubt they will, but if they do, use it, and if your life is seriously in danger, then perhaps you and I will have to meet again, but for now, get out."

She seemed surprised to see the familiar sight of the gas station which she had passed by every day on her way to the school bus stop, a block from her home. She paused there awhile, hesitating. He could almost visualize the thoughts turning in her head as she contemplated how exactly Angel had known her address. She opened the door, letting in a gust of cold air that seemed to break the spell that had incubated the cab just moments ago. Turning and sweeping a stray red lock from her eyes, she whispered:

"Will I ever see you again?"

"Not likely, but I'll see you."

"My Angel," she mused, "the killer chaplain." And just as quickly as she had come into his life, or rather, that he had come into hers, she was gone.

"Bye" he whispered, but the door had already closed.

CHAPTER 2

"THE TRUTH"

He had wanted to tell her who he really was, who he had been and how he had changed ….. the truth. But the truth was difficult to swallow even for himself, better yet anyone else. The truth: he had spent years in prison for a terrible mistake made so many years ago. Back then he had considered himself a revolutionary of sorts. As a youth he had experienced one injustice after another, usually at the hands of some supposed authority. Whether that had been his father, mother, or the local child protective service counselor. Whoever it turned out to be, they all had one thing in common ….. corruption.

In truth, they didn't really care about those entrusted under their care. No, but rather they were all self-consumed with money or strengthening their own positions of power.

Meanwhile, he was left to fend for himself on the streets of Seattle. Ignored by his father and abandoned by his mother, he lived a tragic nightmare far too often repeated in the 'land of the free' until one day, homeless at the age of thirteen, sleeping on a park bench, shivering in the rain, he made up his mind to finally stop being the victim and do something about it. He wasn't the typical thief stealing from convenience stores and shopping malls. Rather, he targeted government run or insured agencies and businesses, such as banks and state run parking lots. All as a form of revenge against the machine that had so ruthlessly steamed over his childhood.

Early on in life he had been tested and prodded by psychiatrists seeking an answer as to why his parents couldn't seem to stand being around him. The results revealed that his parents were simply too impatient to tend to the special needs of a child who was both bipolar and rated a genius on I.Q. tests.

His mother for example, had wrongfully concluded that he was somewhat retarded simply because the things he said tended to be far more advanced than the education she had received. Their oversights Micah then used to his advantage during his one man war against government. Employing tactics learned from video games and spy books, he could often be counted on to be carrying a police scanner and a two-way radio during any particular job. Always one step ahead of the authorities, he became more and more brazen in his efforts, feeling admittedly, invincible.

That is, until that fateful day that would forever change his life and, as it would turn out, hers also.

He had come right at me, Micah thought of the parking lot attendant charged with guarding the fees taken from all of the drivers who parked at the Space Needle for the New Year's celebration fireworks show, having nearly $30,000 in total.

The job really should've been routine. Micah pulls the gun, the attendant hands over the money, simple. But that's not how it turned out. Instead, the clever attendant had seen Micah's suspicious advance using his view through the bubble mirror above him. He took the offensive, heading off the potential robber by jumping Micah before he could pull the gun. Nevertheless, Micah's quick draw caught them both by surprise as the attendant lunged for the gun a few moments too late.

Micah had seen the attendant turn his way and in anticipation of a heroic type move on his part, fired a warning shot in an instant. The warning shot rang off like a thunder clap in the cavernous garage, bouncing off of the walls like the sound of a shootout at the O.K. Corral.

People screamed and ran for cover in all directions while sirens sounded off in the distance. All of which distracted from the attendant lying prone on the concrete.

At trial it was explained that the bullet had ricocheted off of the far wall and pierced the attendant's heart on its return. He died instantly.

The powerful young Prosecutor argued that Micah was in fact an assassin who intentionally planned the death of the innocent man. "Forget that the young man is fifteen" he argued, "a killer is a killer."

That Prosecutor got his wish. He was made famous by the trial and a few months later won the election for Attorney General of Washington State. Micah was sentenced to five years in an adult prison where he languished and plotted his revenge against the lawyer now made Attorney General: Richard Law, famous politician and father of one, Casey Law.

By the time Micah's five years were completed, Richard Law had become somewhat of a small celebrity. Out shown only by his effervescent daughter who always seemed to beam before the cameras. With her easy smile and candid remarks during interviews, she had won the hearts of the Seattleites and neighboring counties, no doubt contributing greatly to her father's political success.

Micah's plan called for a five million dollar ransom. A million for every year he'd spent in prison. Which was fair, all things considered, he thought. But everything he knew of life, of justice, turned on a dime while he was in the process of making final preparations a week after his release from prison.

It was just after he'd picked up the second getaway car, or in this case a truck, that he noticed the magazine article sitting on the passenger side seat that would change his life for good. It was a religious magazine, often distributed by Jehovah's Witnesses, nothing strange there. But the cover story is what had caught his eye that day. Entitled "Can Prisoners Be Reformed?" No, he thought to himself as he hot-wired the truck, hearing the familiar sound of the V-6 roar to life. To him, that sound was what made the job official. Until that moment, that critical moment, it had all just been a plan in his mind. An idea under construction, nothing more. But when that sound emitted from the stolen vehicle it was suddenly all too real, game on, no turning back.

He had stolen many cars in the past for one job or another and this was no different, except he just couldn't seem to shake that question from his mind, 'could prisoners really be reformed?' The battle raged on in his mind while he navigated his way, avoiding police hot spots until finally having had enough, he pulled over to an abandoned parking lot to read, at least the first article.

One hour later he was completely convinced that he had found the truth. Well, at least it was enough information to convince him that stealing a car from a person who was undoubtedly a minister was, at the very least bad juju.

Pulling into the grocery store parking lot an hour later, Micah noticed the unmistakable look of confusion on the face of the old man standing in the empty parking space. Micah pulled into the space as though he were the old man's chauffeur, arriving to take him out for a night on the town. "Sorry for stealing your truck old man," he said as he exited and turned to leave.

"Wait a minute son," he said, holding out his hand.

"What?" Micah retorted, "You want me to give you some cash too? You ought to be glad I even brought it back to you, old man."

"I don't want your money son," he said, pointing to the magazine still clutched in Micah's hand.

"Oh, sorry."

"No, it's alright son. I was just curious as to why you did decide to bring the truck back?"

"Well, old man ...."

"Jeb."

"Well *Jeb*, although it may appear to you that I am just some small time thief, the fact is, it isn't personal."

"Son, it's always personal."

"Yeah, well, let's just agree to disagree."

"It's personal because we are all connected, we are all family and how we treat our family members is always personal. Sure, maybe not to you, maybe not even to me, but to our Father who cares for us both. To Him it is all very personal."

"Listen old man ...."

"Jeb."

"Listen Jeb, my dad don't give a damn about me or about anyone else. Now I'm sorry for stealing your truck but I've got to go now."

"Son, you're on the wrong side of the war."

"Ok Jeb, now you're sounding a bit crazy to me. What war?"

"The war over the issue of universal sovereignty. Angels and demons, good versus evil, God versus Satan."

"Well Jeb, if you guys consider yourselves on the side of what you call 'right', then I hate to break it to you, but you guys are losing."

"Yes son, it appears that way for now, but things will not always be this way. Soon the tide will change, even now the angels are in battle formation in the heavens, poised to strike. Soon everything you know will change. And when it does, you want to be on the right side."

"And which side would that be Jeb? Yours?"

"Jehovah's side son. The God of the universe."

That was the beginning of a conversation that spanned late into the night and on into the following weeks. It became clear to Micah that he had finally found true purpose in life, maybe even the very purpose *of* life.

Unfortunately, those days of being tutored by the old man didn't last long. After just six months of intensive Bible study, Jeb died suddenly of a massive heart attack.

A week after the funeral at the Kingdom Hall, Micah was approached by a lawyer with a sealed envelope. "You were in his will" was all he said, and handed it over.

Inside were keys to the truck.

CHAPTER 3

CASEY'S DIARY
1st ENTRY "POST KIDNAPPING"

Dear diary,

It is 3am Saturday, or I guess now it's Sunday morning. Or maybe I'm wrong about that too as I seem to have lost all touch with reality according to that old hag they call a *Social Worker*. I mean *really*? She had the nerve to tell me that he didn't really exist, that I'm suffering from some sort of P.T.S.D., whatever that means, and that I made the story of my rescue and escape up because children are not yet equipped to deal with the stress. Thus the 'invisible friend syndrome.' And really I don't care how many abused children she has studied in the past who had made up some invisible friend to deal with trauma. It doesn't matter cause I'm different, he was different, and he really does exist. In fact, I can still smell his cologne on my clothes. Angel is real, he is, and he really did save me tonight, or last night, or whatever. The point is diary, that I'm not crazy .... he does exist. They poked and prodded at me in the hospital tonight, stripping me naked and taking swab samples of this and that. In those moments I felt more violated than I did during the entire kidnapping. I found myself wishing that I had never gotten out of his truck, as crazy as that sounds.

I told them over and over again that I had not been touched in that way, but they just kept on testing for this and that, surrounding me dressed up in white scrubs and sterilized boot covers like they were afraid they would catch kidnapping disease 101 if they got too close.

I felt more alone in those moments than I think I ever had before, and that's saying something considering that I practically raised myself while dad pursued his career.

But I guess I'm getting ahead of myself, aren't I? My last entry was what? Four days ago? Yes, four days, remember that I had said that I felt as though I were being followed? And that dad simply ignored me when I told him about the strange van parked down the street? Course that was no surprise, as dad has always been far more concerned with his 'constituents' than he is with the whimsical stories of his eccentric teenaged daughter.

Fact is diary, no matter how many guitars he buys me, I would gladly sell them all if I thought it would earn a donation for his campaign large enough for him to show up to just one of my soccer games. But for right now I would just rather he took my side and believed me rather than that old windbag counselor who spun a story about the condition of my mind not five minutes after meeting me.

Really, dad? You're going to believe the opinion of a stranger you've just met over your own opinion about your daughter, whom you've known since birth? But then that's the real problem, isn't it dad? You really don't know me at all. And Daisy isn't my real mom, she's just the politician groupie of the week, even if you two are married. I doubt Daisy is even her real name, though I did search for it on Google, can you blame me?

Ok, ok, I know I'm procrastinating. It's just that I haven't even settled it down in my own mind yet, harder still to put it down in writing. I'm not even sure I can say it out loud, but here goes! I WAS KIDNAPPED!!!

Now, where do I begin? There were three, no, four of them. They forced me into the van as I was waiting at the bus stop after school, course dad was right about that one at least, as we had argued about the value of my being chauffeured to school for security reasons, an argument that I'd won but now wish I hadn't.

I didn't get a good look at them as they all wore cheap Halloween masks. One was Spiderman I recall and another wore Kermit the Frog. They all smelled like stale beer and cigarettes, and the one closest to me in the far back literally smelled like piss and fear. I remember thinking that I was the one who was supposed to be scared out of my mind, not him.

Anyway, I don't remember anything more of the ride because pee boy put a cloth over my mouth that the detectives said was "chloroform kid, we found enough of it in your bloodstream to kill a 200 pound man. Guess the adrenaline must've saved ya. Yeah, you're one lucky girl." Funny I don't feel lucky. Really, I don't know how I feel exactly, besides tired, dog tired.

One more thing before I end this entry. He gave me a knife. A rather large butterfly knife. That's how I know for sure it all really happened, because it's right here in my hand. I haven't put it down since I got back to my room. It makes me feel safer somehow, I'm not sure why.

CHAPTER 4

THE KNIFE

It was for my daughter, Micah thought to himself as he drove away from Casey that night. What with all the Amber alerts and sickos walking the streets he had to do something to give his daughter a measure of security and himself some peace of mind. But her mother, Crystal, had thrown a fit upon seeing it.

"Are you crazy Micah?! You want to hand that thing to a two-year old child? What? So she can slice her face off? What kind of man hands a two-year old a knife?"

"Uh, the kind that knows what kind of world we live in."

"And what kind of world is that? A world where two-year olds join bike gangs and wear leather jackets? Are you kidding me?"

"Well I didn't mean for her to use it immediately ……"

"No, you didn't '**mean**' to do anything. You never '**mean**' to do anything, but still, somehow people get hurt around you, don't they Micah?"

She knew of course that he had a dark side to him that he was struggling to keep under control, but until then she had kept it to herself. "As long as you come home to me baby" was all she ever said to him whenever he was walking out the door wearing all black 'and looking dubious.'

She was a good woman and mother to their child until she died in a car accident while Micah served his prison sentence.

Angel, their daughter, had been taken by Child Protective Services while Micah was told to 'stay away' now that he was a convicted felon.

He always knew that in his line of work something bad may happen one day and that's why he'd decided to create a clever tracking device so that he would always know where she was.

The homing beacon only activated while the knife was in the open and locked position. However, in addition to the beacon was a miniature microphone that allowed for the receiver to pick up all sounds within a ten foot radius, all of which was programmed to alert Micah's cell phone once activated. The screen would flash the words "ANGEL …… ANGEL ….." and then a GPS screen would appear, pinpointing the knife's location while giving full audio.

But that wasn't even the feature Micah was most proud of. What he loved most was the borrowed technology from a series of 'momentum' watches. Micah used these ideas in the construction stages of the knife. Now, when the knife was opened and the handle swiveled, the device would recharge itself continually. Right now all of that technology, (really, Micah's best yet invention), was in the hands of a seventeen-year old girl. A girl that had no idea what it could do. But he knew that if he got the call one day, he'd have to find her again, in hopes that, somehow, he might restore some of the peace that he once, so long ago, planned to take away.

CHAPTER 5

CASEY'S DIARY ENTRY 2

Dear diary,

Went to school today, if you can call it that. It was more like a circus and I was their freak. Cameras followed me as I mounted the steps into the main hall. I'm used to the cameras of course. As far back as I can remember I was being filmed in one way or another, from my first steps to dad's first political campaign. But this was different. Back then I was the young starlet and the reporters all clamored as the flash bulbs popped. I glowed under daddy's prodding. But now the lenses seemed cold somehow. Mean and skeptical, as though they were all waiting for me to freak out or fall down and burst into tears. But I wouldn't give them the satisfaction, no, not a single tear.

Besides, dad and his newest friend 'old hag' had vehemently advised against my coming back to class so soon, feeling that the added pressure of school work and the media, would impede my progress to 'normalhood.' Not only did it give me great pleasure to defy the old woman, this was the only place outside of my room that I felt truly normal .... as normal went for my life anyway.

The familiar buzz of the first class bell, the clanging of the locker doors, even the awful smell of the ladies room .... it all screamed 'normal' to me, even if the teachers looked at me with puppy dog eyes and spoke to me as if I were sitting in a high chair adamantly refusing a serving of peas.

It all didn't matter to me. I am out in the public, not hiding under the apron strings of a mother I didn't know.

'Live your life without fear' he had said in the truck. Well I'm living Angel .... if this is living. But then really, what else could I do?

Talked to Sam today, (she hates to be called Samantha even though I told her a million times that the rumors saying that she was gay would only continue if she keeps calling herself Sam). But then, what do I care what she calls herself. As long as I can depend on her to believe me when no one else will. But I guess things don't always turn out to be as you'd expect. I finally got her alone in the ladies room after first period ended. "So I know you've been waiting, so just go ahead, ask Sam" I encouraged her.

"Go ahead ask what?" she asked, putting on her best innocent face.

"You know, go ahead and ask me all your weird questions about the abduction."

"You're calling it an *abduction*?"

"That's what it was Sam, an abduction."

"Yeah, but you make it sound like some aliens came down and stuck a probe in you or something."

"Whatever, just ask your questions,"

"Well, what if I don't have any questions?"

"Sam! Stop acting weird."

"Weird? Why is my not asking questions weird?" she asked as a crowd was beginning to form around us.

"Well Sam, if you were Billy Bob Nobody then I suppose it wouldn't be weird, but considering that you are the editor of the school newspaper and my best friend, you'll have to excuse me for thinking that you may have some questions."

"You're making a scene Casey. Maybe you should've just stayed home like the psychiatrist said."

"How did you know there was a shrink?"

"You see? That's what I mean Casey. Everybody knows and we all just want what's best for you." Yup that was about all I could take of school today. It was obvious that dad had gotten to her and given instructions to handle me with kid gloves. And even though she nodded when I told her about Angel, I knew she was just placating me, as by now she normally would've torn me to pieces with obscene questions as to 'whether he was handsome' and 'maybe you've finally found a boyfriend who can keep up with you, even if he is a stalker.' Clearly, she had been briefed.

No matter how many times I told her that I was ok, even in my best Katy Perry voice, she just kept on looking at me as though she had just received her masters degree in psychology and was about to be the first one to discover some new type of delirium.

As for the rest of the kids, they just stared at me as usual. All their suspicions finally came true.

'Little Miss Know It All' finally got into a fix even her daddy couldn't save her from. In their eyes every 'A' I ever received was because daddy's security detail had strong-armed the teacher in some dark alley the night before the test.

And even if I got a 'B', it was only to throw off the suspicion of the others so that they didn't discover the St. Mary High conspiracy going on under their noses. Some even felt that the entire kidnapping was, in fact a publicity stunt, set up by my father's shrewd campaign team. After all, who wouldn't vote for the poor father of the now mentally damaged starlet?

Sometimes I wish I had been adopted by some Australian couple in the deep outback and my only worries were of being run over by a kangaroo or chased by a croc. I would run around and say things like 'crikee' and 'g'day mate.'

But no luck there, instead I'm just some disturbed rich girl who was probably just violated in ways that even Sister Mary Thomas herself wouldn't dare to repeat. In fact, the only real excitement I got today was when I snuck past the new metal detectors in the hallway. They'd probably break out the straight jacket if they'd have found the butterfly knife in my purse, sitting in my secret pocket along with my Berry-Pink lip gloss. Passing to the side of the metal detector must've seemed warranted to them anyhow, as 'Big Tom', my dad's most intimidating bodyguard followed me right to my first period class even though I argued till past midnight with dad that this would only make me look more conspicuous. But of course, he wouldn't relent, saying that 'this is my one condition' and throwing the whole 'taking the bus to school' argument back in my face.

Big Tom never speaks, at least not to me. In fact, the only time I've ever seen his mouth open was last Thanksgiving when he swallowed an entire turkey in one long, continuous bite. I'm not even sure he has any real fighting skills. He's just a big hulk of a man, threatening sub shops from here to Manhattan.

I don't know why I thought of him just now.

Angel .... what if Angel and Big Tom were to have a run in? Angel, if you are out there, I'm ok, I'm safe. But if I start looking like a meatball sub, then you'd better come running. Angel, who really are you? A remorseful kidnapper? A bounty hunter? No, you'd have used the front door. That and you didn't smell like piss and cigarettes. You smelled more like that cologne that was popular in the nineties. What was it? Eternity? I'll never forget his voice. It was soft but not weak. Confident and self-assured but somewhat compassionate. It was almost as if he knew me personally. Do you know me somehow Angel? A friend of my father? How did you know where to find me? A private detective, maybe? CIA? But then I noticed an Awake! magazine in the truck. How funny would that be, a Jehovah's Witness CIA agent! Now that is funny! Probably wasn't even your truck, was it Angel? Seemed like an old man's truck, not what you'd expect from a dark ops agent. And what did you mean "I'll find you?" How exactly can you do that? Unless of course, you were watching me all along, even today possibly, hidden amongst the crowd of reporters. "Angel …. Angel …. Where are you now?"

CHAPTER 6

MICAH
THE DAY AFTER

She changed shoes. Either that or the tracking device in that particular pair has short circuited, he thought to himself. Either way it's no longer getting a signal. Didn't matter anyway, she was streaming live on every channel. He could just stay there at the bar and watch her on TV while he decided what to do about the getaway kidnappers.

CNN kept showing the same footage of her taking the authorities back to the warehouse, retracing her steps and answering questions from the detectives. Strangely, she didn't seem to be the usual shook up victim typically associated with these sort of crimes. In fact, her nonchalant description of the events seemed to miff even the most seasoned crime investigators, causing some to suspect that she had some involvement, perhaps a desperate cry for attention. Either way, it was quickly becoming one of the most famous cases in American media history, complete with bloggers logging in to vent their frustrations or pose new conspiracy theories. Riveting T.V. for sure, but while the cameras were following her around he would have to occupy himself with other media reports as he was sure that the kidnapping crew would have to generate cash quickly to compensate for their losses.

One news story seemed promising. There had been a robbery in Salem, Oregon just a day after the botched kidnapping. It was a team of four that were partially caught on camera but there wasn't a clear enough shot of any of them to narrow the search. Nevertheless, Micah was familiar with their tactics, and as soon as he saw the footage of the lead robber wearing a police scanner taped to his chest, he knew he had found his men. They must've gotten desperate, well, he thought, more desperate than usual. Two of them were compulsive gamblers and were probably up to their necks in debt to the local loan sharks. Micah finished his beer and tipped the waitress as he made final plans to leave for Salem. He had no idea what he'd do when he found them. He doubted knocking on their hotel room door and offering a free home Bible study would help.

Normally, he wouldn't chance leaving Casey alone in the city so soon after the event, but she had a semi-truck of a man following her around that he figured to be a secret service agent or security detail of some sort.

Besides, with all the media following her she should be perfectly safe for a while. That is until Britney Spears or some other fame goes on a bender worthy of drawing the public's eye. He didn't figure the boys would make another attempt as there was now no money in it, still, with these guys it was best to make sure there wasn't anyone holding grudges.

On the positive side, he didn't believe that the fellas knew that it was him for sure. It was far more likely to have been a private bounty hunter paid for by her father, or at least that's what he hoped they thought. Course, there's a chance they recognized the truck. He knew he should've used a stolen car or something else but it had all happened so fast that there really wasn't time for thorough planning. Besides, with his new found faith he was at least going to make a go at trying to fly straight.

As it was, he did get to her in time. She seemed no worse for the wear, scrappy little thing that she was. He still couldn't fathom why she hadn't jumped out at the first red light once they were clear of the district. He hated to indulge theories but it was almost as if she trusted him exclusively from the first words whispered in her ears. Who knows? Maybe she was just too terrified to run, afraid that he'd just turn the truck around and catch her again.

In any case, it was clear that she hadn't told the detectives about him or the knife as there was nothing about a 'rescuer' in the news, and truth be told, Micah had listened in on her prayers the last few nights as she seemed to have formed a habit of playing with the knife at night.

In any case, he thought, it was nice to hear her voice. "Well, I'm going to Oregon, Casey," he whispered to himself, "but don't worry, God is watching and his tracking devices are far better than mine."

CHAPTER 7

THREE YEARS LATER

The phone lit up, "ANGEL ...... ANGEL ….." nearly jump starting Micah's heart while toppling him from his chair as he sat behind his counter in the video section of Radio Shack.

He hadn't heard from her in three years but from what the papers had said, she had been in and out of counseling for the first two years, but things had leveled out as of late. Something to do with a 'new religion'. Nevertheless, the call was real, although the audio was somewhat muffled by the sound of an engine. He believed he'd heard at least two other girls with her and the GPS indicated that they had been in the same spot for quite some time, somewhere near Tucson, Arizona or just south of it near the Mexican border. The same area incidentally that reports a high amount of sex trade abductions.

He drove all night, worrying and listening for clues of troubles until he came upon the scene. He pulled up driving his new Jeep expecting some sort of chaos, but instead he found them in full spring break party mode, stranded on the side of the road in the middle of the Baja desert, fifty miles from the border. Three girls and a 'frat boy' if he had to guess, whose party had been interrupted by a flat tire that frat boy was now trying to pry off of its rim using, of all things, the butterfly knife.

"Hey, that's not the right tool for that!" Micah said, climbing out of the Jeep wearing a ball cap and reflective sunglasses. He strode over and snatched the knife from the bewildered young man and handed it back to Casey, a move he realized all too late as being highly suspicious. He was acutely aware that she was now locked on and staring at him in much the same way as she had back when he'd asked her to trust him while wearing a ski mask. In fact, it *was* the same sarcastic expression as she was now shooting his way. Fortunately the spare tire from the back of his Jeep fit perfectly on their Chevy Blazer. Her friends insisted that he take their twenty dollars for the tire but he simply tipped the brim of his cap and said "Y'all be good, ya hear." What an idiot, he thought to himself, but he couldn't think of anything else to say. She was making him nervous and imitating the Southern voice of his grandpa seemed as good as any at the time. "Wait a minute," Casey called out from inside the truck. "Don't you want *your* knife back?"

"What you say na?" His accent was getting worse.

"I said, do you want your knife back?" she repeated, tilting her head to peer around his glasses. "Ha, na y'all youngins' take care of dat one der, she sounin' bit loo na." And with that he turned and got back in his Jeep.

She was just as beautiful as he'd remembered, although it's true that the camera really does add ten pounds. Still, she had the same powerful effect on him as before, tilting him off balance and challenging his every word.

Usually he felt powerful and in control of his surroundings and circumstances, yet, somehow she had a knack for turning that upside down.

As he drove away he couldn't help but feel like she was still watching. 'Man Micah, you've got to be smoother than that,' he chided himself. He had given the knife right to her like an idiot. He was trying to take some comfort in the fact that technically he had had a one out of four chance of guessing whose knife it had belonged to and that they'd probably thought it was a coincidence he'd handed it to her, but of course Casey was right on top of it from the beginning. Smart alecky and sharp, she didn't miss a beat. But who knows, he thought, maybe grandpa's accent saved him.

CHAPTER 8

CASEY'S DIARY
ENTRY 230

Dear diary,

    Well I'm glad I took you along for spring break as the strangest thing happened today. Sam, Christina, Ronald and I have been stranded on the side of the road now for two days, until guess who came? I was really beginning to worry as we were running out of bottled water (that thankfully I had insisted on bringing as you can never trust the water in a Mexican Hotel.) Anyway, we had popped a flat, though genius Ronald had said we didn't need a spare as they were 'run flat' tires. Last time I listen to anything he says.

    Truth is, I hadn't even wanted to go on this trip in the first place. The awkward feel to it had all begun with our argument over the tires three days before.

    "Run flat tires are only good for like fifty miles or so Ron. What if we pop a flat out in the middle nowhere?" I argued.

    "Casey, you're such a kill-joy aren't you?" Sam interrupted.

    "What does my comment about the tires have to do

with being a kill-joy Sam? I'm not saying I don't want to go, I'm only saying we should take precautions."

"Precautions for what Casey? Huh Casey? Why don't you just say what you're really thinking?"

"What are you talking about Sam?"

"Oh you know exactly what I'm talking about. You're paranoid! Even your dad and your psychiatrist know it, I don't see why you can't. This is why no one wants to hang out with you. You think those kidnappers are going to somehow miraculously escape from prison, drive down to Mexico, throw some spikes in the road and 'ABDUCT' you again, all just so that your pretty face can be all over the news again. But I've got news for you little miss paranoid. You're not as cute as you used to be. You're getting old. What are you? Nearly twenty-one now?"

"Ok. First. Harsh Sam that was really harsh bringing dad and the psych into it. And second, yes I may be a bit edgy, but the news said that they only caught three of them ….. and rumor has it that there were four or even five …..."

"There were three Case, just three ….."

"No. There was at least one more."

"So what? There's four of us and only one of him,

correction, five of us if you include your imaginary friend ….. what …. Angel was his name?"

"Ok, now you've gone too far Sam ….."

"No. You Casey. You're the one who always goes too far and this is no exception! Now I've been patient with you for three years now. Haven't I been patient? But now you're ruining my vacation with your incessant worries and fantasies thinking that you're the center of the universe. Honestly, I wish you'd just shut-up ………"

"Shut-up?"

"Yes, Shut-up. Why is that such a big chore for you? It's over Casey. The kidnapping is over. The cameras have stopped rolling, the world has moved on and it's high time you do so too. They're not coming back for you, he is not going to save you again, if he even exists in the first place. It's time you let it go."

Yup, that's how our trip began. I should've jumped out of the truck before we got up to speed, but apparently that is a skill I have yet to master.

So there we were three days later, stranded on the side of the road, with me holding back the biggest 'I TOLD YOU SO' in world history when all of a sudden we see this red Jeep cresting the hill heading in our direction.

So let me set the scene. Sam, Christina and I are in the truck, windows down in the blazing heat. Ronald, against all my protests, is using my knife like a crowbar trying to pry the tire off its rim, and up pulls this Jeep. Now here's where it gets crazy. Out jumps this Ray Ban wearing Mexican or possibly Islander from Texas or somewhere south judging from the accent, if in fact it was his own, which of course makes me sound crazy if not viewed with all the other evidence that I will now provide.

So as I said, he jumps out of the Jeep and says something like "What are you doing to that knife?" I know right? I mean, here we are stranded and dying of thirst in the middle of the desert, sweltering away in the heat of the day and all this guy cares about is the knife. And immediately I think .... Angel!

I know, I know, we were past all of that fantasy stuff, but just let me finish. So he takes the knife from Ron and hands it to me through the window. CAN YOU BELIEVE IT! I mean, you couldn't make this stuff up if you were writing a book, right? So he's got this spare tire on the back of his Jeep that *just so* happens to fit perfectly, and he just hands it to us free of charge. I mean, who does that? And diary, I swear he was intentionally trying not to look at me, I mean it was obvious. And the glasses, did I mention those goofy glasses? I mean, they didn't even fit him, in fact, they still had one of those UV stickers on the lens as if he'd just bought them for a disguise. Coincidence? I think not. But that's not even the icing on the cake. When he said good-bye he all of a sudden had an accent. An accent that didn't exist when he was yelling at Ron about the knife.

So, the verdict? It could've been him.

I know, I know, I'm going to drive myself crazy again. After all, every bus boy, storekeeper and cab driver was Angel for that first year or so. Still, this was different. I guess in that first year of therapy, I just assumed that Angel would have to have been nearby if he was going to save me in a pinch. Therefore, it was logical to conclude that he would occupy a job of that sort, at least as his cover. But when I sprained my ankle while jogging that first year and had to drag myself nearly three blocks to the nearest hospital, well, to say the least that broke the spell a little on the idea that he was nearby. Course, any girl foolish enough to go jogging alone without a cell phone these days could be labeled crazy just for that.

Dad had long since given up on my sanity before that anyway.

The 'old hag' had convinced him that some people never fully recovered from a trauma like mine and that by the looks of things he should be thankful that 'she's at least somewhat functional and has friends' which many victims did not. I guess that's why he didn't complain much about my becoming a Christian, as at least I had some new friends. Besides, it was true that most kidnapping victims are never found .... alive anyway. So if I had survived, then it had to be for a reason.

Maybe God was directing my life in a new direction, who knows. But that magazine in Angel's truck had sparked my curiosity, no, not about religion, but rather whether or not he could be found at one of their services.

So, naturally when the Jehovah's Witnesses came calling, I was all ears. Funny thing was, I found that we had something in common. Most everyone seemed to believe that the religion was filled with brain-washed followers and of course I had become 'Queen of the brain-washed' as of late, so it made for a perfect fit. Nevertheless, I found them to be quite reasonable, kind and their diligent use of the Bible intrigued me.

On the subject of paranoia, I don't really feel as though I am paranoid, or scared for that matter. Three of the kidnappers had been caught using marked bills from a bank robbery just a week after the news broke of my recovery. Apparently someone had tipped off a casino in Oregon about the circulation of marked money and so they had been caught at the Black Jack table after the dealer became suspicious about the rather large sized bets they were placing.

They turned on each other less than a week after the trial began and I guess one of them made a deal with the Prosecutor to testify against the other two, although all three swore that it wasn't their idea. We all watched the trial develop from home as they said that my testimony would only be needed if the men didn't plead guilty. I just closed my eyes as the defendants were being introduced and listened for Angel's voice among them, but was quite sure he wasn't.

About the fourth kidnapper. He is still at large and for some reason the other three refused to give any information about him. But I can't live in fear. I was a prisoner for nearly two days, I won't let it become more than that by letting them steal my heart too.

So, anyway, maybe it was Angel today or maybe it was just a Good Samaritan. Either way, thank you, whoever you are and may God bless you.

CHAPTER 9

RADIO SHACK

He saw her today. True, he'd seen her all the time on TV, some E Channel special about 'Kidnapping Survivors and Where Are They Now?' But today was the real thing. He saw her face to face, no mask. She must be what, twenty now? She strode into the store with her main girlfriend in tow looking for a new rechargeable battery for her laptop. And where better to get one than Radio Shack?

It was the only legitimate job he could get with his criminal record and so he'd been working there for the last four years, much to his disappointment. It didn't pay the best but it had its perks. For example, they carried all the latest spy ware, every- thing from night vision goggles to listening devices and mini cameras. Not that he'd ever need the goggles but one never knows.

In truth he wished he could just quit and move to California (where he'd heard it's always sunny and dreams come true). A place he'd visited as a kid. But as things were, one of the conditions of his custody hearing to win back Angel was that he 'maintain stable employment in the state of Washington.' Then, if some counselor agrees, he might be awarded partial custody. For whatever good that would do as she was already thirteen years old now and probably hated him. Who knows what those foster-parents were telling her about him. Whatever it was it wasn't good, as Angel had yet to return a letter to him in the last few years. Anyway, that's what he was thinking when Casey approached the counter.

"May I help you?" he said professionally, as she laid the computer down.

He had of course noticed her from the moment she'd walked in the front door. (How could he not?) Not just because the manager Bajwa was constantly reminding them to "be a salesman, remember our promotions and talk to them as soon as they walk through the front door."

No, it was for the same reasons that it had always been with her. It was because of the curly red hair that bounced off of her shoulders as she walked and the way it just seemed brighter in any room she entered, or maybe the sheer force of her personality had simply altered the way he'd previously viewed beauty in general. Either way, she had it, whatever it was. In fact, everyone seemed to notice her, proven by the fact that Ronnie, a skinny twenty-year old wanna-be rapper, jumped right on her with a sales pitch about some 'half off speakers.' She turned him down flat before he could grab a microphone to show her 'how much bass these puppies put out' and thank God for that as Micah had heard that gangsta rap one too many times. It was too bad he didn't have friends close enough to tell him he wasn't black. So there she stood before him in person, her hand on the counter just inches from his, while she glanced at the phones in the display case, a moment frozen in time, until her friend interrupted.

"Well? Are you gonna just stand there or get her a battery?"

"What?" he fumbled, "what battery?" Casey smiled.

"She said she needed an ultra-life battery. Hello, is there anybody in there?" her friend retorted.

"Be nice." Casey counseled, "He probably couldn't hear me over the sound of that rapper." Her sarcastic smile lit up as Ronnie hit his second line, "Yo, Yo, put your hands in the air."

"Yeah," Micah continued, "he's sorta like our mascot being as the Seahawks Eagle asked for too much money. That'll be fifteen dollars."

"Well," she said, "somebody oughtta warn him not to try out for American Idol."

And just like that, with a smile and a flip of the hair she was headed out the door serenaded with the lyrics "Yo, Yo, third verse same as the first."

CHAPTER 10

CASEY'S DIARY
ENTRY 250

Dear diary,

Today is my twenty-first birthday. Not that I celebrate birthdays, but for me this is an important time in my life. I'm thinking of marrying Ron, whom as you know is a solid man and spiritually sound, not to mention rather cute. Really, I've been debating this decision for well over a year now and the thing is, I love him. I'm not 'in love' with him, but I care about him a great deal and I expect that the love will grow over time. Sometimes that's good enough, right? But there's a problem as you know. The same problem that I've had for years now. The knife. It's not that it's a dangerous weapon that technically a Christian shouldn't be carrying around, no, it's deeper than that.

It's what it represents. Anything can be an idol, for example, if it's put before God. So money could be an idol or food can be an idol. It's not the actual object or goal that makes it that way, it's the way you treat it, the time you sacrifice to that object of veneration. For me, although the knife is not an idol, it represents everything that I am trying to move past.

Every session with a psychiatrist, every news report about being a victim, every sleepless night wondering if he'll come. It represents a man who does not exist, at least not if I'm planning on having a normal life. And let's be honest, how can I fall in love with someone when in truth I'm already in love? CRAZY!!! I'm in love, not with a man, but with the idea of a man. An idea fabricated in my imagination. Now how crazy is that? The knife has in effect stood in the way of every meaningful relationship I could've had. It is the visible manifestation of my dilemma. A dilemma that has to end, must end.

So tonight I'm going out with the girls for a drink, just one, maybe two. I'm going to enjoy myself like a real person. I'm going to celebrate the new me. And in the morning I'm going down to the pawn shop and that will be that.

CHAPTER 11

YAK

His phone lit up just a little after midnight Friday. Anxiety marched into his mind like enemy soldiers, as immediately he knew this call was for real.

For one thing, the GPS location beacon was moving at a high rate of speed just outside of Seattle and heading south towards Tacoma. She must've been in a vehicle of some sort but judging from the muffled sound of her voice and the all too familiar beat of the "WU-TANG CLAN" rap group blaring over the stereo he knew it wasn't her vehicle and she was most likely gagged. As he rode his Ninja motorcycle south bound on I-5 at speeds cresting 120 mph, he couldn't seem to get one name out of his head. A name he hadn't said out loud for years. Yak.

He had good reason to worry. If it was him, if it was Yak, then she was in serious trouble and probably had very little time left. He had first met Yak in the weight lifting room in prison. Yak was on his back bench pressing four wheels, that is to say 405lbs, over and over again. Micah wasn't the only person to take notice of the incredible scene. The entire gymnasium had fallen dead silent, as though they were all witnessing history in the making.

Slowly someone behind him began to count: "10, 11, 12 ..." soon they were all counting: "14, 15, 16 ......" He made it to 20 before he calmly racked the bar back into its place above his head. As he stood up it seemed as though he were riding in a glass elevator getting taller and taller until finally he stood a full six foot seven inches tall.

It reminded Micah of the stories told by his old history teacher, stories about the mystical Auroch, a bull the size of an elephant that he asserted went extinct during the gladiatorial games of ancient Rome. He had said that the disposition of the bull was like no other, unstoppable, fierce and determined. He had said "the only way to beat it was to get out of its way."

That was Yak. A black man with a barrel chest the size of a V-8 engine and arms like the support beams of a beach front pier.

People, including Micah, parted before him even before he motioned in their direction, all of them trying to guess which way he'd go next and always conscious of where he was in the room. In the cafeteria, he could usually be found at a table by himself, eating two or three trays of food. No one ever asked where he got them. Officers stood to the side as he passed, not wanting a conflict.

Once, it was said that he'd seriously injured another convict during an argument about toothpaste. When the officers came to his cell and told him to turn around and 'cuff up', he simply said 'no' and the officers, not knowing what else to do, just left.

When being transported from one prison to another, Yak was restrained in three pairs of handcuffs, as he was known to easily snap a pair or two if he was in the mood. All of this power and blind rage was thus contained in a man with the nickname 'Maniac Yak' or 'Yak' for short.

It took nearly two weeks before Micah finally got up the courage to talk to him, but ultimately, he needed his muscle for the plan. In a year, Yak would be released, so why not use him, Micah thought, at least then he wouldn't have to carry her.

The problem with Yak was, that no one knew his true motivation, it wasn't money. His latest crime had been in robbing a jewelry store, tying up the cashiers and simply leaving. No theft of jewelry or cash, which was why he was getting out so soon. That's why, Micah guessed, he wasn't caught at the casino with the others when he had given that anonymous tip to the authorities.

In fact, had he to bet it, Yak was probably at the local strip club at the time of their arrest, handing his bank marked bills to unsuspecting girls whose love of money overrode their fears of approaching the hulk of a man in the far back corner of the room.

These memories fresh in his mind, it wasn't long before Micah caught up with the speeding utility van advertising 'Locksmiths and Windows, we'll see you through the pane of locking up.' Well, if it was Yak, then 'pain' was definitely in the picture. Stolen of course, as no sane business owner would hire him to make keys for strangers' homes. In fact, it wouldn't surprise Micah if the actual owner was lying dead somewhere on the side of the road.

He couldn't see anything through the rear window but there appeared to be no movement inside other than the driver. Pulling into the left lane, he sped past the drivers side window. Yak! There was no mistaking him. His hulking shoulders filled the side window as the steering wheel was all but completely hidden under the grasp of his massive paws. He wore no mask, so whatever he was planning to do with her, he wasn't afraid of being identified afterwards. An ominous sign.

Micah began front trailing the van. A move he'd learned from watching too many Bond movies. It was a move where the trailer car stays in front of the vehicle being followed to throw off suspicion. Then using the mirrors to watch for the turn signals of the vehicle behind, the lead car could quietly stay in front.

It was a move that wouldn't work if the mark driver didn't use turn signals, but thankfully Yak was the model driver, careful not to draw any unnecessary attention from the police. Eventually Yak pulled into an abandoned parking garage in the Hill Top area of Tacoma.

There was nothing slick about what Micah did next, as he pulled right into the garage with them, turning off the bike and dismounting right in front of the now parked van. Taking off his helmet, they met eye to eye in the beams of the van's headlights.

The door cracked open as Yak stepped out, the van lifting up having been relieved of his weight. It was as if the car had hydraulics, which would've been cool, Micah thought, if we were at a car show. But as things were, it looked as though this scene would end with first place going to whomever could walk away afterward.

"She's mine," Micah growled under his breath, as he side-stepped the open door a few feet from Yak's grasp while trying to get a look inside.

"You had yo chance boss, now she mine," Yak countered, reaching for a crowbar on the passenger seat.

"You know you'll never get away with it," Micah argued while circling to the back and catching his first glimpse of Casey through the rear window. She appeared to be passed out, possibly dead, but from the way Yak spoke of her, she was probably drugged.

"Why? Whatcha gonna do boss, phone in an anonymous tip? Sides, who said I'z tryin to get away?" he taunted calmly as he walked to the front of the van. They stood facing each other with the hood of the van between them.

Quickly, Micah pulled on the handle of the passenger door yelling "Casey! Wake up!" but it was locked. Unsuccessful, his efforts delayed him long enough for Yak to run around the front of the van and, lunging, took a swipe at his head with the crowbar, barely missing, but instead smashing the side mirror clear into the passenger side window, shattering it in a hail of glass. Micah ran to the rear doors. Again locked. This time Yak didn't miss, slamming the bar into his ribs, evoking an involuntary '*yelp*' while spinning him to the ground in pain as he rolled away from the next blow that clanged onto the concrete, showering sparks into the cool night air. Remembering his childhood judo lessons, Micah jumped back to his feet, ignoring the sharp pain, circling back to the front of the van. "Casey, wake up!" his voice now barely a whisper as he struggled for a full breath. Waiting for Yak to commit to following him to the same side, Micah sprinted around the front once again. Reaching through the broken window, he popped the lock of the passenger side door. Launching himself inside, he grabbed for the first weapon he could find and while turning onto his back, threw it at the oncoming bull.

The flashlight bounced off of Yak's face like a toothpick as he reached for Micah's ankle, dragging him back out. Grabbing the steering wheel with one hand, Micah used his free one to fire a newly found lunch box at his face. Yup, that slowed him down, Micah thought, as the edge of the steel container slashed open Yak's cheek, loosening his grip on the ankle as Micah kicked free once more.

"What? What's going on mom?" came a weak voice from the back.

"Casey! Just drive, DRIVE!!"

Yak labored to regain his senses on the ground just outside of the open door. Micah jumped out, retrieved the lunch box and began arcing it up for another blow. Course, he should've just left well enough alone as the next hit came suddenly. It took a minute to register that the blow had come from behind him, from inside the van.

"*Casey*? What?" Before he could figure that one out, another blow came from down low, connecting with his shin, sending him toppling down to Yak.

"How'd ya like dat one boss?" Yak chuckled, as he regained his crowbar.

"What's going on?" Casey asked, stooping between the driver's and passenger's seats, looking at the two of them in confusion.

"DRIVE CASEY!!!" he screamed out, somehow recovering his voice just as he felt the next blow glance off the side of his head, partially deflected by his raised arm fending it off.

The van roared to life and began to pull away, nearly running over Micah's outstretched hand, but successfully colliding with his motorbike.

"Gotta go boss," Yak quipped as he broke off his attack and threw himself partially into the open door as the van picked up speed, turning toward the entrance.

His long legs and massive feet dragged along the ground as he tried to pull himself inside. Nearly halfway in, the van abruptly turned hard left toward a support beam, smashing first the door, then Yak, into the concrete pillar. The door came wrenching off of its hinges, loudly screeching its protest, finally separating, cart wheeling it and Yak to the ground. Micah gingerly rose to his feet, looking on in consternation as the van turned the corner, then suddenly stopped in the middle of the road some twenty yards away.

She stepped out of the van and turned to look at him as he stood hunched over holding his side. He couldn't tell whether she was just making sure he was down or making sure he was alright, but as their eyes met, it appeared that she finally knew which of them was the enemy.

Suddenly her gaze turned, drawing Micah's also. Yak was gone! Micah immediately braced for the blow, swiveling around to intercept it, but no blow came. Yak was gone. The fading taillights were all Micah could make out before she disappeared around the corner, heading toward the freeway, and just as quickly as it had all begun, he was once again alone.

Micah's mother had always been against his purchase of the motorbike, saying it was 'death on wheels'. And although he had always disagreed with her, that particular night he wished he'd listened as the pain was excruciating just trying to keep the bike upright, on the ride home.

Twice he laid the bike down at dangerous speeds scraping his shins on the roads as he maneuvered the darkened streets back to Seattle. Can't go to the hospital, he thought to himself, as there'll be questions, questions and more questions, most of which he couldn't answer if he were to have any chance to gain back custody of Angel. Ultimately, the night ended with him dragging his bruised and broken body up three flights of stairs, finally reaching his low rent studio apartment at the top.

He laid there on top of his blankets staring off into the ceiling until he at last drifted off for the rest of the night and well into the next day.

When the returning pain finally awoke him at six in the evening the next day, he instinctively reached for the cell phone. The screen was dark and clear. She must've closed the knife, he reasoned, but perhaps a new chapter had just opened.

CHAPTER 12

CASEY'S DIARY
ENTRY 251

Dear diary,

I am never, ever drinking again. It was my first time but apparently alcohol and I don't mix. I'm not even sure where to begin this entry. There are two versions of this story.

First, I'll give you Sam's take. According to Sam we were all at a bar in downtown Seattle having a drink. Then a giant black guy offered me a free drink for my birthday as it was announced by the bartender after he read my I.D. Of course I said no, politely, but when I did it didn't seem to register on his face. He just stood there over me and Sam as if it wasn't a request. Well, I thought, one more drink wouldn't hurt as I had barely even touched my first. Besides, it seemed the only way to regain our private conversation.

Now so far both mine and Sam's version are identical, but what she says happened next is where our stories differ.

According to Sam, I then drank four more shots of Tequila, even against the protests of both Sam and Christian, and then, (here's where the story gets really weird) I apparently asked that same guy for a ride to the pawn shop. Now as to how my supposed friends would possibly allow me to get into the car of a complete stranger I do not know. "You looked like you were having fun", said Sam to my question. You see, this is the problem with having friends who do not share your morals or principals.

There's no telling where they will draw the line if you don't. More on that later, but for now I'll finish her version.

He instead drove me directly home, using my ID for directions as I had apparently blacked out or passed out on the way to the pawn shop. Sam then later stopped by my apartment to check on me and I was safe and sound at home already asleep by the time she arrived at 1 a.m.

I cannot begin to tell you how many things are disturbing about this account, but that's not what bothers me the most.

What bothers me is that my version is far more disturbing, if not outright nightmarish. It is important to note that I have absolutely no proof of what I'm about to say but for the sake of sanity or maybe proof of insanity, I will divulge all that is in this young corrupted mind.

Ok, so remember the black guy? Hard not to as he was nearly seven feet tall and probably ate small children for a lunchtime snack. Yeah, so I remember the drink he bought me .... all clear so far. But that's about it for the bar scene.

The next thing I know, I'm dreaming of my mother, my real mother. We are out in a field in the summer, surrounded by pink and yellow flowers that for some reason smell like WD-40. I am three or four-years old and my mother is taking fresh laundry off of the clothes lines and handing them to me saying "take them up Casey, take them up." The fresh smell of sheets and daisies full of WD-40 fills the air. Then mom turns to me and yells "They're dry Casey! They're dry dammit!" while holding up a long white sheet. I say "what mom?" then she screams "DRIVE CASEY, DRIVE!!!"

Suddenly I wake up into another dream. Now I'm in the back of a van laying on top of some tools and broken padlocks scattered everywhere. I see light ahead so I move towards it. It's light coming through a windshield, so I stand up using the headrests for support. The right side passenger door is wide open and the black guy from the bar is about to be killed by some maniac wielding a lunchbox. So I threw a padlock at him, connecting with the back of his head. That did it, and suddenly I see him buckle from the blow and collapse. Then I tried to ask some kind of question but no voice came out. I hear mom screaming "Drive Casey! Drive!!!" So I jump into the driver's seat and start it up putting it into gear.

We're in some kind of a parking garage and suddenly I feel the van lean down hard on the passenger side. He's halfway out of the open door hanging onto the seatbelt. I think to myself, 'boy, he's really scared for his life'. I reach out to help pull him in but he's too heavy. He grabs my arm, fear in his eyes, but his weight jerks me and the steering wheel hard right. I look up and see the post too late, jerk hard left to compensate and that's when it happened.

I didn't actually see the impact, but I heard and felt it. It was like I'd hit a deer with a Volkswagen, taking the door clear off of its hinges. My heart dropped into my stomach as I pulled free, hearing nothing now but the soft breeze rushing through the vacant doorway. I turned the corner and was about to drive away when I heard a voice whisper "wait for him". So against my best instincts I stopped and got out, crazy as that may seem.

And then I saw him. Clear as day. Angel. Standing under the lights of the garage looking straight at me. I can't tell you exactly how he looked, except that he was shorter than the guy with the sunglasses near Mexico. It's possible though that he was leaning down somehow, which would explain it. We stood there for a while just staring at each other. Blood ran down his face concealing half of it, but it was him, it was Angel. Then for reasons I can't explain, I simply got in and drove away. I drove straight home and parked out front.

Anyway, I woke up this morning and checked for the van out front. Gone. Now I could've called the police but what was I going to say that would *not* end me up in a loony bin? 'Hello, Police? Yes, apparently I'm losing my freaking mind and would you please direct me to the nearest funny farm?'

What am I going to do diary? Am I losing my mind …. again?

One small note to add. When I awoke, the knife was no longer in my purse but rather sat closed on my lamp stand. Needless to say, 'butterfly', no pawn shop for you until I figure out what in the world is going on.

CHAPTER 13

MICAH'S RECOVERY

He did of course wind up in a hospital bed the following day. The results of the x-rays found two broken ribs on his right side, a fractured tibia in his left leg, sixteen stitches to the forehead and back of the head (the last one thanks to Casey) and deep subcutaneous bruises to the right forearm, left ankle and lower back. Good news was he could still walk even though he would have to wear a protective boot for four to six weeks. However, these things were the least of his worries.

First and foremost on his mind was the worry that Casey would go to the police and reveal, by means of a sketch artist, his identity. With computers these days, it was possible that it would be enough to match to his juvenile file, leading them directly to his place. Second among his concerns was that Yak was nowhere to be found. It was important that Micah find him as it was now clear that Yak had plans for Casey that didn't involve her living the rest of her life in peace. Either way, last night's encounter was too close for comfort and humbling to say the least. Up until that moment, he had felt somewhat in control of the situation. But Yak made clear that he needed to step up his game if her were expecting to come off victorious. In fact, had Casey not woken when she did, they would both probably be at the bottom of Union Bay by now, or worse, tied up and alive in some dungeon awaiting their fate at the hands of a madman.

He had been watching the news from the emergency room waiting area but had not seen that anyone was aware of what had happened. But it was hard to think about such things as he writhed in pain.

Really, how had this gotten so out of control in the first place? Did he really need Yak to pull off the plan of the kidnapping? Or was there more to it than that? At fifteen was he so timid in prison that he felt he had needed Yak to help him just to survive prison? No. He was terrified. To be honest, he never really forgot it. How could he? No one forgets their first day in prison. But especially not him as he had barely survived his second. It was as clear as if it had all happened just yesterday.

The gleaming steel razor wire coiled itself in circles above the chain linked fence. An endless line of miniature stakes dotted the fence top at intervals.

He felt his heart seek refuge in his stomach as the bus pulled to a stop inside the gated checkpoint. From the small slits in the windows he leaned in and glimpsed the gun towers looming over the prison, like giant bullies poised to hunt down anyone running, like rabbits. He strained against the cold shackles to get a better look at his future home.

Inside the fence line loomed a fortress of concrete and iron. Barred windows lined every building and structure. Large plate signs identified the closest structure as cell block R-4, the next as cell block R-5.

He wondered if tiny faces were watching them come in from behind those darkened windows, wondering, just like them, who they might recognize among the groups of chained convicts.

He saw fear and anticipation in some of his bus mates eyes. A whole range of emotions rolled through him as the prisoner in front of him pulled on his chains as they headed off the bus.

The sun blinded Micah's eyes and the smell of pine assaulted his nostrils while he took in the scene.

Armed guards were yelling out directions as the convicts milled into the concrete building. A cold gust of sterilized smelling air hit him as he followed through the door, sensing a point of no return.

The room was laid out in a long hallway separated by chain link cages that lined one side. In one cage at least 30 men stood naked, nervously shifting their feet while trying to cover up their private parts. The cage past that one held men in various stages of getting dressed, all donning huge pumpkin colored one-piece jumpsuits. His group however was being led into the first cage, reserved for those due for a buzz haircut. The guards said something about precautionary lice prevention.

Taking comfort in numbers, most of his group shuffled toward the back of the cage, no one wanting to be first.

One by one they were unshackled. He bent down to scratch the indents in his ankles where the cuffs had dug in.

This had to be a bad dream. Maybe this was just some test, some pre-emptive scare tactic to keep them all under control. But the cold of the room made reality hard to ignore. The smell of their bodies a foreboding indication of the future.

After a year of sitting in a county jail cell he had become an expert at waiting. After all, that's really what prison is, various stages of waiting. Waiting for a release, waiting for parole, waiting to die.

He was just sentenced to serve five years in a hole just like that one, so he guessed he'd better get used to it.

There are things that the public doesn't know about being inside a place like that. Civil rights lawyers would have a field day if they knew just half of the atrocities being committed within those muted walls.

For so many years he breathed the unique air of a wanted fugitive fraught with danger and hope. Then suddenly at age 15 there's nowhere to run. The anonymity of the outside stripped down to 'height, weight, criminal history.' No, he was not walking away from this one. He made a silent prayer to God. He wasn't particularly sure if he even asked for anything, he just wanted someone to talk to. To feel not so alone at that moment.

Naked underneath his pumpkin suit and trudging the yellow painted hallways he found his way to the back end of the group. "TATE, 7-9-8-4-8-7, T. A. T. E. front and center." The officer looked over the group as he came forward. "That you? Well here, take this bed roll and report to cell block R-4." He handed Micah a roll of bedding consisting of one brown scratchy wool blanket, two sheets and a pillow case. No pillow. This is it.

Micah was soon to meet his cell mate.

Young and afraid, he only hoped that God would not leave him to fight for survival amidst some lunatic's idea of a welcoming party. But the cell was empty when he arrived. Probably because whoever it was, was eating chow. So he headed on down to the chow hall.

The large room was one of the largest he'd seen yet, with more convicts freely moving about in that space than he'd thought safely possible. If it weren't for the pumpkin suits, he'd have been convinced that he'd just found the food court of a super mall.

Looking around, he realized that groups must have formed sometime while he was in his own mind. Or perhaps they had been there for much longer than himself.

In any case, he picked up his tray. Mashed potatoes, gravy, a thin slice of turkey, some stuffing and corn on the cob. No seats seemed to be saying to him 'Hey, Micah! Sit here, it'll be alright." So he circled the water fountains while keeping his eyes open. He had to sit somewhere soon before it became obvious how afraid he was. So he simply chose a spot, sat down and began cleaning his plastic ware with a paper towel. One never knew how clean those things really are.

He was aware of who was sitting around him but made no eye contact. He simply picked up his corn on the cob and took a bite. He watched it sail through the air across the table. A kernel of corn that had escaped his cob as he'd bit into it. They all watched it going in slow motion, bent on its crooked path. A bald man's head made a target too tempting to pass on. Yes, the world was conspiring against Micah. It was his first day in prison, his first real meal.

He'd been trying to make a statement by choosing the table occupied by possibly the most menacing black man on main line. Taking a cue from his bravery, two scared to death convicts had joined him. They all saw it happening, eyes locked onto it as though a car crash in slow motion.

With a wet sounding 'smack' it landed dead center. The man looked up from his mashed potatoes, face impassive, eyes black as death. "Sorry man, my bad." Micah didn't think his voice had cracked, but it may have. The man reached up with a massive hand and, locating the kernel on top of his gleaming, bald head, glared at Micah while flicking it aside. Micah had heard everything that man had said to him in that moment, although he never opened his mouth. When the man refocused on his potatoes, Micah took it as his cue, his shoulders relaxing as he went for another bite.

Micah began to think of his short-lived life as the next kernel flew. What are the odds he'd die like this? No daring stand-off with the police, no wailing sirens or pursuing cars. No. Micah's end would come at the hands of a turkey dinner. The moment the man opened up to take a bite of the stuffing, it landed. Smack dab in the middle of his tongue. Both of Micah's companions shot up and backed away from the table. His hands gripped the edges of the table. Like a scene from a Bruce Lee movie, the man spat out the kernel in disgust and turned to stand up, glaring at him, poised to attack. Micah's hands shot up, palms out like a 'crossing guard.'

"Wait! Wait! It was an accident." For a moment he just stared at Micah with a deadly glaze forming over the whites of his eyes. Then, as if pardoning a serial killer from the judge's bench, the man went back to eating. The rest all stayed put, suspicious of his calmness, but eventually, hunger won over fear and so they finished their meal.

The man was an immigrant from an African country who'd managed to find his way into this madness, just like Micah. In fact, he sat with Micah every day after that. He wasn't much of a talker. Everything Micah knew of him had come through the prison grape vine. A week after that first day they had their first real conversation.

He'd never forget it. They sat in their respective places as usual when out of the blue he said "Can I read that book after you?" Micah was stunned, guess he didn't expect such good English coming from him. "What book?" he'd said. "That book you're reading to your cellie. You know, I'm three cells down from you and I can hear you guys clear as day. You're reading some book about Shadrach, Meshach and Abednego," the man replied, seeming genuinely interested. "Sure, that's the Daniel book we're just about finished," Micah had answered.

Thinking about it all now in the hospital waiting room he realized he had been afraid. But not just that. Somehow he'd totally forgotten about his first real contact with Jehovah's Witnesses. It had been in the form of that book. The Daniel book.

It was all beginning to make sense to him now. He was 15 years-old, desperate and confused. He had seen many religious books lying around prison. It seemed everyone in prison was keen to suddenly find religion. The hypocrisy of it all repulsed him at the time. But in that particular prison there were no T.V.'s in the cells, no radios.

He'd found the book simply lying among a stack of others and was drawn to it. Skepticism and doubt were always his first defense to religion, but this book was different. It out rightly admitted that many skeptics criticized the Bible book of Daniel and went on to furnish convincing archeological proof of its inspiration of prophecy.

Really, it was the first time in his life that the stories in the Bible looked less like fairy tales and more like true history. Of course, it wasn't enough to convert him. No. Nor did it stop him from fabricating a scheme to kidnap Casey. Jeb would have to do that later.

But it did explain why the magazine in the truck had such an effect on him and also further explained why he'd needed Yak. After all, they served corn on the cob every Sunday and he'd have five more years to do. All in all, it was an answer as to why he was now here at the hospital. Really, it was a mix of faith and fear, now mingled with pain as he sat there waiting to be seen.

Further, (and this could be the pain talking) it seemed counter intuitive to have a waiting area for an emergency room. Wasn't the point of coming in this wing the fact that it could not wait?

First question. "Nature of emergency?"

Hmmm. "Pain." Micah responded with a roll of the eyes.

"And how did it happen?" she prodded further.

"Ummm, motorcycle accident," he said, justifying that at least it was the cause of some of the bruises.

He left the hospital and went directly to his religious service that evening. The public talk was entitled "Love for Enemies." A lecture that had him squirming in his chair throughout. How could anyone love Yak?

AGENTS OF TRUTH

There exists, hidden deep in the shadows of twilight, in the alleys rarely traversed, just before the breaking of the sun, those agents of TRUTH who carry the scars of the night before. We are heard about in the silence between lovers on a subway car all but empty except for them and me. These agents of TRUTH walk among you during the daytime and greet you at places of business and are for the most part, normal to all appearances.

Then one day, while dicing tomatoes for dinner in your 'art-deco' kitchen you hear the news reporter announce "Breaking News."

Someone has done something unimaginably bold. So you move to get a closer look at the television, and there he or she is. That same one who said "have a nice day" as they bagged your tomatoes just moments ago. And you say to yourself, "I wonder what that person was really like in private?" Well, I am he. I set the balance that makes the universe equal itself out. I help you appreciate every day you breathe above ground. I am one of many. I am an Agent of TRUTH.

A Poem by Yak, age 6

CHAPTER 14

BACK TO WORK

Bajwa, his boss from India who had risen through the ranks of Radio Shack, had decided not to give him a day off for his injuries as he'd said, "It is no like you are lumberjack. You sell batteries and cameras, you don't need two feet for that. Look at Ronnie, he don't have half a brain, still, he sell more than you."

Being back at work again was nerve racking and tedious, not to mention that he was high on the narcotics given to him at the hospital. It was yet another bill he couldn't afford.

He did however, have the presence of mind to surf the net for the last known address of Yak. It was high time he got out of reaction mode and into prevention mode as someone once said 'the best defense is a good offense.'

Not surprisingly, he found that Yak's last known address was Tibet. And that in fact, he is an ox that stands five feet tall at the shoulders and is harvested for his long wool coat every summer. Searching further, he found three strip clubs that were listed in the Hill

Top area. With a few well placed calls, he found a patron matching Yak's description that often frequented De Ja Vu.

Obviously Micah couldn't simply stroll in and have a little chat with Yak. No, he thought, this was going to take a little more planning than that. Tomorrow he would have to pay a visit to the establishment early in the morning in hopes of both avoiding Yak and possibly finding a dancer with enough free time to give him his address if he made it worth her while. Or at least he hoped that's how it would turn out.

Anyways, that whole 'what if' game rolling through his head combined with the pain killers kicking in was what kept him from noticing her as she walked through the front door.

CHAPTER 15

CASEY'S DIARY
ENTRY 252

Dear diary,

Ron proposed to me today. I know, I know, I have been waiting and dreaming about that moment ever since I found mom's old wedding dress in the attic back when I was 5. But the way he did it wasn't quite as I'd seen it in my head. He just sort of mentioned it mid-sentence over the phone just after asking if I drink coffee with or without cream. Crazy right? He said something like, "Well, these are things I should know about you if we're going to be married." Yeah. Sam couldn't believe it either. But I don't want to be too harsh, after all, he isn't the real problem anyway, I am.

How can I give myself completely to a man when I don't feel complete myself? Further, he has no idea the depth of my delirium. In fact, neither do I. But after today I'll know for sure. I hope. So I decided that to be fair with him and to myself I had to say no. True, the way I said it could've been done differently. I think I said something along the lines of, "Tea. I've always had tea Ron. Please tell me that what with all the times we've been to Starbucks together you at least noticed that I have never, ever, ordered coffee?" I know he didn't deserve it and that at a later time I will need to give him a better explanation. But what was I going to say "Ron, I think I have a split personality disorder and only half of me thinks that you and I are a good idea?"

Anyway, as big as that situation was, Ron wasn't the real reason for this entry. Today is about the other name that keeps rolling around in my head that keeps popping up at night robbing me of sleep and testing what's left of my sanity.

So, Angel, if you are out there, I'm tired. Tired of playing games, tired of sitting here waiting for either the next foot to drop or for the answers to simply fall into my lap, making sense of it all. A girl wants more than just breadsticks and water. Sooner or later the main course has to arrive.

Today I became pro-active!

First stop, Radio Shack. If I'm going to do this then I'm going to do it right, no half-stepping. One thing I did learn from my father is that if you're planning on going down the rabbit hole to find Alice, then you'd better record every moment on film for fear she will disappear into the night again and no one will believe you.

Or maybe it was his shrewd campaign manager that had said that back when dad was accused of secretly fathering two children at once by different women. Either way, I needed a new camera.

Preferably the 'see-in-the-dark-waterproof-impact resistant-can't-break-it-if-it-was-runover-by-two-semi-trucks-locked-in-a-death-match' model. One never knew what to expect with Angel, he had an uncanny way of appearing out of no-where.

That thought in mind is probably what kept me in the 'night vision goggle aisle' a bit too long. Not as though I could afford it. Sure, dad had given me my own apartment on Queen Anne Hill and a limitless credit card. But the words 'limit' and 'less' were the words dad had stressed in that sentence.

Besides, an eight-thousand dollar charge to his card for 'goggles' was sure to draw his attention which would lead to questions that at present I didn't have answers to.

"Yeah, I've been eyeing them too" came a voice from behind me. It was the cashier from the other day. I don't know how he snuck up on me with that big plastic boot on his foot, but he was sorta strange anyway. He looked terrible. Not that he had been a 10 to begin with but he wasn't bad looking from what I remember.

Today however, he was sporting a new haircut, and that's the best I can say about it because actually he had all of his hair except one long patch shaved bald dead center and an impressive row of stitches decorating the landing strip.

"What happened to you?" I asked, trying to go easy.

"You" he said with a wry smile.

"Nice pick-up line. But seriously, what happened, your house cat get outta control?"

"Oh you know, all of us Radio Shack guys double as secret agents in the night."

Yeah, clever I thought. It must be some predominant gene that all men have that prevents them from telling the truth. Although, admittedly, he did it with a bit of charm.

Really though, there wasn't any doubt as to what had happened to him. Judging from the last time we'd spoken, he was anything but smooth, sort of clumsy but in a cute way. People like him sustain major injuries from things as simple as getting caught in revolving doors.

Unlike my Angel, who seemed impervious to pain once he set his mind to something. And yet, even though I knew he had issues, he made me feel safe somehow.

Anyway, the cashier went on to show me a large variety of cameras, big ones, small ones, ones for underwater filming. Something about his voice was calming but we were interrupted by 'Yo, yo, here we go ....' Not again. I guess that customer didn't want the speakers either because he stopped before the third verse, which if I recall, was the same as the first.

"So what will you be using the camera for, *sexting*?" he asked jokingly.

"Ha, ha. No, my plans are far more sinister than that. I'm going to Hill Top to an abandoned parking garage to see if I can find evidence of an abduction," I said with my best Katy Perry voice. I guess it wasn't a very good imitation because at that moment his whole disposition changed.

I mean, one moment we're bantering back and forth, even flirting a little and the next moment it was as if he couldn't get rid of me quick enough. He just sort of bagged up the camera without ceremony and said, "Well, thank you for shopping Radio Shack."

Weird, really weird fella. To add to his weirdness, as I was leaving he asked for his break and left in a hurry out the back door as if he'd just received an emergency call from some hidden earpiece. And just like that I was back in my Jeep heading south on I-5.

When I arrived at the parking garage, (which I was happy to find did really exist, at least proving to some extent that it wasn't a dream but that I had really been there.) I expected to find blood, broken glass, maybe a marked off crime scene under investigation, but sadly, none of that was there. No glass, no blood. There were peculiar marks on the cement support beam that (if it was true) I had struck. But to be honest, it wasn't very convincing as I checked the other beams and they'd all seemed to have been struck at one point or another. It's something but certainly no smoking gun. And there was glass but not nearly enough to make up for an entire broken window, which could be accounted for if the window had shattered inward leaving most of the glass on the seat, but now I'm reaching a bit. I walked around for a while filming the lot which was completely void of cars save for one red Jeep. The same type incidentally that had been driven by the Mexican sunglass wearer back at the border. It was probably stolen as it was clearly out of place for that neighborhood. Didn't matter much as I believe Angel had ridden a black motorbike of some type. So in effect, there was no evidence. So it didn't happen Casey, it was all just a dream.

You've probably been here before at some point and you simply remembered this garage into your dream. Unless of course, a street sweeper cleared out the garage, which Casey, is definitely reaching and completely implausible given the amount of trash and aluminum cans lying around.

People really should recycle. According to the Bible, one day everyone will recycle and the whole world will become a paradise, but right now it is anything but a paradise. Instead, it's as if we've used the earth for our own personal latrine. In fact, that very garage was like a microcosm of the world.

The dank smell of urine, evidence of illegal activities, graffiti scarring the walls with every unclean thought and depraved saying. Yeah, I had to get outta there.

What I did notice however, was that there were cameras mounted in the corners of the ceiling. Perhaps they had recorded the entire event. Course I'd have to pull a few favors to draw that kind of information and I think I know just who to ask. Scott. Dad's campaign manager.

CHAPTER 16

MICAH AND THE GARAGE

You have no idea how difficult ordinary chores like sweeping can be while wearing a plastic boot, Micah thought. His only saving grace had been that there wasn't enough blood to have required a mop or anything major. Just a few drops of blood here and there which he, in desperation, to get it cleaned up in time, peed on, to wash it away. Ah, the cleaning power of urine, which in ancient times was used for all types of remedies and medicinal purposes.

So, other than that situation, the cleanup went smoothly considering the short time he had to finish the job before she arrived.

He was just loading the mangled van door into the back of the truck when he caught a glimpse of her rounding the corner. With barely a second to spare, he launched himself into the back of the Jeep.

Landing on the top of the van door with a thud, evoking an involuntary gasp, the impact, a cruel reminder of how a place as benign as the garage looked at that moment, just the other night was nearly the scene of a murder. His own.

He'd always known that asking for tinted windows when he'd purchased the Jeep had been a bit pretentious, but at the moment, with her so near, milling about with that camera, it was now his only cover. It's hard to articulate the effect she has on him, he thought, as he rubbed his bruises. Even in these moments, when she was, admittedly, looking a bit disheveled.

The 'I just woke up' look seemed to work for her. He wanted so badly to just jump out and say something like, 'So, are you busy tonight, cause I know a great tea and sushi joint.' But it could never work. They were from two different worlds. A convict and a politician's daughter? Yeah, right.

The simple fact is that all solid relationships are built on honesty and trust. How could he ever explain who he is, who he was and what parts of the old him still remained? And her father, what about her father? No doubt he would remember Micah. And although Micah wasn't prone to being afraid of any man, still, her father had the law on his side. It wouldn't be too far-fetched for her father to invent charges against him if he flatly refused to stop dating his daughter.

Yet, she was worth the risk, as he'd proven last night. But would she accept him for who he was? She was in fact, too good for him, he knew. Which perhaps was the real reason he hid in the back of his truck as she looked for proof of his existence mere feet away.

Sometimes who you hope a person is, is much greater than they actually are, or perhaps ever will be. She was hoping to find a hero, but he was in fact, a villain trying desperately not to let the clouds of his past forever darken the skies of his future.

Also, and if he was being honest with himself, she hadn't exactly jumped all over him with interest back at the store. Granted he looked as though he'd been in a plane crash, but even those times before that, when she'd visited the store, she'd shown no real interest then either. Perhaps he just didn't have the look that a girl of her caliber went for. Enchanting as she was, surely she had her standards, standards that rose high above an ex-convict.

They stayed there like that for nearly an hour. One of the most difficult of his life. Separated only by his timidity and a tinted window. Then she seemed to look up as if she were praying for answers. Perhaps she was giving up? Maybe? But he had to admit, it was probably for the best. Moments later, as if she'd somehow come to some sure conclusion in her mind, she got back into her car and left him there. The vacancy in his heart was palpable. She left, and somehow it felt as if she were leaving for good. She was gone, and with her the answers to the questions burning in his heart, but now, were far too late to ask.

CHAPTER 17

CASEY'S DIARY
ENTRY 253

Dear diary,

Scott was a dead end. He said that it would require a court order to pull the footage from the security cameras at the garage and he felt that my new interest in cinematography was not going to be enough leverage to convince a judge, no matter who my father was. But it doesn't matter anyway. Went to Sam's wedding today as the maid of honor. But it didn't feel like an honor at all.

Instead, it was more like a funeral for my dreams and a depressing reminder of how far I had traveled from reality. It wasn't just that I could've been that girl up there, glowing before her man dressed all in white because really I think I always knew I couldn't marry Ron. No, I guess what it was, what hurt the most, was when I was asked to smile for the photos, but each time I tried it became harder and harder not to burst out in tears. I wanted to be happy, and I was happy for her as I want nothing better than for her to have her dream life. It's just that I had seen something in Angel, or who I believed him to be, that made it impossible to settle for less. So who would I ever marry? What man is going to risk his life for me and carry me out of danger in his arms? When and with whom would I ever feel that confidence again? I was truly myself with him.

And maybe it wasn't so much him as it was with who he helped me to be. He didn't treat me as my father's daughter or the media's darling. He cut right to the core of me with a word, and straight to the soul with a touch. Lost. That's what I was at that wedding. Lost and confused. Why does it feel like I've just lost the man of my life when I never actually had him?

This morning Seattle felt its first frost of the winter. As though I needed another reminder that my love life has less heat than the Alaskan Highway in winter. In fact, mine is more like the iceberg that sank the Titanic. Not only am I cold and frigid, but I wreck even unsinkable relationships, like mom and dad's. It's no mystery why they broke up after I was born. Maybe I was simply born for misery, masked and hidden in the many papers of their divorce.

In fact, the only positive thing that came out of that wedding was that by proxy I was finally given an answer to my problems. It was when the new husband

and wife were taking their ceremonial first dance. Someone asked me to dance also, but I guess the expression on my face said it all, although I didn't mean to hurt his feelings. It was right about then that I heard someone whisper behind me, "Why did she even come? She should've just stayed home. People like her are destined for loneliness, she should just leave instead of bringing the rest of us down." It cut like a knife .... but it was the truth, harsh as it was, that I needed to hear. I need to go. I don't remember much of mom as she stopped visiting back when I was young. But one thing I do remember is that she always said she was the happiest in her life when she was sitting under the warm sun on the white beaches of Santa Barbara, California. She'd said that time had stood still for her there. That clarity was only possible once you'd first appreciated the little things. Like the surf rolling in under a cloudless sky pushing the cool sand between your toes. Clarity. That's what I need right now. Because even though I feel more me when I'm with him than at any other time, and to be honest, maybe he helped me to find me in the first place, if that makes any sense. Still, what defines me cannot be someone or something other than myself. Maybe he was my rebound dependent. Fled from being daddy's little girl, the media's little darling, to Angel's little damsel in distress.

I've got to face the facts. Angel does not exist and my belief in him has ruined even my relationship with myself. At this point you could put me in a room by myself with nothing but a mirror and I'd get into an argument. I went to the garage and didn't find anything. Nothing. It simply didn't happen Casey. It was a dream within a dream.

I've gone as far as I can go with it. I went down the rabbit hole and came up empty. And now what am I? I'm just a broken wind-up doll that's been left in the toy box because I only spoke one phrase, 'ANGEL .... ANGEL .... ANGEL...'

Maybe, just maybe, I've become just what the old hag had said, never to work right again. Well before that happens I've got to give myself one last chance to live, to really live. A famous poet once said, 'the best way to predict the future is to invent it.' So that's what I'm going to do, re-invent myself.

First, I'm going to cut and dye my hair, then, it's time to move. The simple fact is, everywhere I turn to in Seattle and now Tacoma, I irresistibly look for him. Hoping that he's around the next corner or maybe the lifeguard at Alki Beach. So I've decided. I'm moving to Santa Barbara. If mom found clarity, then maybe I can too.

VOLUME II

CHAPTER 18
MICAH'S VACATION

Santa Barbara was a beautiful town. Filled with blossoming cherry trees and manicured parks lined with palm trees. It was what the prisoner next to Jesus must've envisioned when he was told he would soon be in paradise. Micah remembered what it was like to be a prisoner himself, and he too hoped to find relief here. Course it'd been Angel's idea originally.

Now that she was eighteen and legally able to be with her ex-con father, it was where she wanted to vacation. She'd said, 'it's the perfect place to relax and get to know you.' Course, it didn't hurt that the Red Hot Chili Peppers were playing L.A. that summer.

In the end, he never did win custody of her. He'd shown up in court bruised and beaten just a few days after the garage incident. The Judge took one look and decided that he hadn't changed a bit. If only she knew, he thought. A shame really, as he had had the support of his congregation there in court, testifying in his behalf.

It had been a painfully honest moment for him that day, humbly listening to his criminal record read out loud in front of so many persons he'd grown to love and respect. When he'd heard the final judgment handed down, it'd struck him like a punch in the stomach.

He went on to lose nearly twenty pounds in the weeks that followed, much of that weight in tears alone, he imagined. But now she was here with him in person. So he had to be grateful for that. Even though she'd made it clear that she needed a friend more than a father at this point.

He'd always wanted to move to a place like this anyway and thanks to an unexpected bonus check from Bajwa, he could now afford to move here if he so chose to. It turned out that Bajwa had been a far more savvy businessman than anyone had given him credit for. That whole time Micah had worked at Radio Shack, Bajwa had been selling products imported from India on the shelves, which, as it turned out, was completely legal and extremely profitable. He retired of course and left Ronnie and Micah the shop. 'As an inheritance,' he'd said. He always had treated them as though they were his own children.

Watching the sun set into hues of pink painted clouds had a way of making him feel at home even though he was miles away from her. Casey had stayed with him, in his mind and heart, everywhere he went. He found himself, even now (two years since he'd last seen her back at the garage) checking his cell phone, half hoping it'd light up and she'd have need for him again. Even if she'd just open the knife to play with it, at least then he'd know where she was. Even the media couldn't seem to find her.

Angel liked California too, although she says it isn't her first time here. A comment he was too afraid to follow up on. She drew the eyes of everyone, wearing her new bikini. Another argument he'd lost. Eventually, she cut him deep, saying, 'just because you sired me doesn't make you my father!' She had a quick temper and refused to give his religion a chance, but what could he do? Ultimately she was the product of what he'd failed to be as a father. He had the feeling she was just, in her own way, trying to protect herself anyway. She'd been disappointed and abandoned so many times before by people who claimed to love her, she wasn't going to be quick to take another chance with trusting someone proven to leave at the drop of a dime as she saw it.

The first weekend in Santa Barbara turned out to be a game of chase with her running away and him trying to warm up to her, but she seemed to have locked nearly every door to her heart. He even went so far as to bring her out for ice cream, desperate as that may seem. "I'm on a diet dad. You don't get a body like this eating Krispy Kremes and Baskin Robbins. In fact, you could use to lose a few pounds yourself dad."

Don't know what she'd meant by that. He'd always thought he was in pretty good shape for thirty-two, but what was more important to him was that she'd finally called him 'dad.' It wasn't much, but it was a start.

Angel wandered into the ice cream parlor while he basked in the moment of 'daddy-ism' out front. Perhaps he wouldn't have noticed the beautiful woman with the short black hair, were it not for the Watchtower magazines she was offering to passers-by in front of the store. But had he not, it would've been a mistake, as her beauty was without parallel in his opinion.

Noticing his gaze, she turned and looked at him quizzically.

"Daiquiri Ice?" she asked.

"Hmmm?" He stammered.

"Daiquiri Ice? The flavor of the ice cream you're holding."

"Oh. Of course. Ice cream. Yeah, it's my favorite flavor."

"Mine too."

"Really?" he asked, surprised.

"No, not really." She laughed. "And what is your *girlfriend's* favorite?" she said, looking at Angel through the window store front finishing her order and coming their way.

"Oh. Uh, she's on a diet." he said as Angel came out front, seeing the two of them and rolling her eyes.

"Well," she continued, "have you ever wondered what food would taste like if it were all natural, you know, without all the preservatives?"

"Well yes." he said, pretending not to catch on to the direction of the conversation.

"You know, the Bible promises that one day all things will be made new and that everyone can sit under their own vine and fig tree. Do you think you'd like to live in a place like that?" she asked.

"Well, I don't know what kinda shade I'm supposed to get from a vineyard, but ok I'll bite. Where do I sign up?"

"He's a *Jehovah's Witness*." Angel blurted out, having had enough of the conversation. The lady turned to him, face flushing red and smiling from ear to ear.

"And just how long were you planning on letting me go on like that?"

"And I'm not his *girlfriend*, I'm his daughter. As if!" Angel interrupted again.

"Ok," he answered, a little bit off balance, "guess the cat is out of the bag. Don't get me wrong, I wasn't like, intentionally trying to deceive you. It's just that you were on such a roll and it was a different approach than I'm used to, so I figured I'd just see how long it'd take you to get to the point."

She eyed him suspiciously, then slammed a fist into his shoulder, laughing.

"Besides," he continued, "I think I'd probably listen to you regardless of what you'd have to say." It was his best attempt at a line yet, he thought, and he'd have to give himself the old pat on the back later if it worked.

"Oh give me a break," Angel retorted, "I'll be waiting down the street at Macy's, dad. Come get me when you're finished embarrassing yourself."

"So ….." she paused, leading ….. "you just visiting or staying awhile?"

"Um, I'd like to stay ….. wait, how'd you know we were tourists?" he asked, trying to recognize if he'd seen her before.

"Let's call it an educated guess. Besides, it looks as though you're going to stay," she said, motioning down the street to where Angel stood flirting with a Mohawk wearing young man.

"Anyway," she continued, "I hadn't seen you at the local Kingdom Hall, so I figured you must just be passing through."

"How do you know for sure I haven't been there yet? Isn't it possible that I was there just last Sunday and you just didn't notice me?"

"No," she said definitely, "I'm quite sure I'd remember you, had you been there. Although I'll bet if you had come you wouldn't have remembered me."

"No. I'll bet I'd know your face anywhere," he said, still trying to place her face.

"Be careful what you bet brother. I'd hate to have to call you on it."

"Ok, let's say somehow you're right, but one thing's for sure. I'll never forget your name."

She paused for a moment uncertainly, looking him over, then finally answered, "*Sheila*. My name is Sheila.

"Well Sheila, I hope to see you again. I'd better get going before my daughter makes me a grandfather," he said jokingly.

"You'll see me at the Kingdom Hall right?" she asked expectantly.

"I'm afraid not, as I attend the Spanish services. But I'll find ya, it's a small town," he said with a wink.

"Oh, are you Latino?"

He paused there for a while, finally remembering her features in his mind. Then slowly, deliberately, closed the distance between them, grabbing her waist and motioning as though he intended to kiss her. Not pulling away, she instinctively turned a cheek as he whispered softly, "No .... *Casey* ..... I'm not ....." He stayed there, close, feeling her breath raise the hairs on his neck, while tenderly tracing the line of her jaw with a touch. Drawing back and peering intensely into her eyes, he slowly began to pull away, releasing her at last. And with that, he turned to leave, already planning for the next time they would 'run into each other' again.

CHAPTER 19

CASEY'S DIARY
ENTRY 400

Dear diary,

Somehow, someway, I should've known it. It was all right there in front of me. The bruises and scars he carried in the store the day after the garage, the protective boot on his leg. He even told me back then that the reason for his injuries had been "you" and still, somehow, with all of that I never suspected it. Granted diary, I have dropped some pretty big bombs on paper since that psychiatrist suggested that I start writing this diary, but this tidbit of info went off in my head more like a Chernobyl meltdown.

Radio Shack Guy ….. is …… Angel ….. and what's more, he is here now, in person. I recognized him from the store immediately and was, to say the least, surprised to see him so far from home. Course, I suspected right away he'd followed me somehow, and that 'somehow' could be because he knew or worked with Angel. But as we stood there conversing on the street corner, he seemed to subtly change right before me as if I'd somehow caught him off guard and out of costume. Possibly because his beautiful daughter was there and he'd had no time to 'get into character' so to speak. All of which were thoughts I was pushing back in my mind trying to find another solution, anything really, other than to say his name again. And then, suddenly, he made that graphically impossible.

We're out in public, people milling about everywhere as we talked. Then, seemingly out of nowhere, he pulls me in close. And then it's just us. No people milling around ….. no sound of traffic passing by ….. suddenly the world around me disappears with no one left but him and me. And I knew it was him ….. only Angel had that perfect balance between power and grace that could shut out the world around me.

When I was a kid there were all those stupid vampire movies where the helpless girl just lays there and lets him bite her, and I always thought 'why aren't you fighting for your life stupid?' But at that moment, wherever we happened to be when he held me in his arms, I finally understood. Such is the hold he has on me. Has always had on me.

To add to the bomb dropping news, he is also a Jehovah's Witness, which if we're keeping track, rules out Navy Seal, CIA, and possibly even Bounty Hunter.

Leaving only private detective or kidnapper in my rolodex of possibilities.

I'm still trying to place it all in my mind and to be sure, now that he's here I'll have a lot of questions. But for now I have at least one answer. I'm not crazy ….. never was. But to be honest, it wouldn't have bothered me if I was. One thing these last two years of solace has given me is the peace of knowing that I'm ok, even if I am a bit crazy, who isn't? And what with all the brides-to-be passing through my floral shop, I've come to realize that I'm not alone shopping in the crazy section of the mall. So tonight I'm going out. To a barbeque held by Angel's longtime friend Mike, who said "glad to finally meet you in person. I was beginning to think you weren't real from the way he spoke of you."

"Yeah ….. I know the feeling."

CHAPTER 20

SUNDAY'S SERVICE

Micah sat quietly in the far back row vainly attempting inconspicuousness.

Two things he could always count on with a Jehovah's Witness service. First, that no new person goes unnoticed and ungreeted. Second, no matter where he went on the planet, regardless of language, the subject under consideration was the same everywhere simultaneously. A comfort to him given that he'd only studied for the session in Spanish. He took out his Watchtower and read along with Emerson, his best friend, whom they had been staying with while visiting town.

Michael Emerson was nothing if not consistent. A mid-thirties Caucasian with chiseled looks and serious eyes, he had forever been Micah's only confidant. Emerson had moved from Seattle years ago in hopes that Micah would soon join him, but the custody hearing had taken longer than either of them had expected and now he had been there waiting long enough to master the art of surfing and hang-gliding. The latter of which, he whispered, had been a matter of concern among the elders. Sanctity of life was a big Bible issue, a fact that Micah needed no reminding of.

Nevertheless, risk somehow always seemed to find him and that risk invariably went double when Casey was around. He scanned the crowd to see if he could find her, finally locating her near the front row. She was just as he'd remembered, beautiful and articulate, a fact revealed when she raised her hand to comment on the 'facets of Daniel's vision .....' and whatever else she said coming out like a song in his ears.

He sat there wishing that his daughter had agreed to come, but there was no wrenching her away from Mohawk, who wanted to show her *the pier.* She'd already seen enough 'piers' in his estimation. "Seattle's waterfront is dotted with piers, Angel. Why come all the way to California to see another one?" he'd pleaded to no effect.

The service ended quietly with Emerson pulling Micah down the aisles toward the exit, explaining there was little precious time to prepare for the barbeque that Micah would attend 'without option' tonight.

CHAPTER 21

CASEY'S DIARY
ENTRY 401

Dear diary,

Barbeques have never been my favorite occasions as I have been a vegetarian as long as I can remember. Dad always said, 'you'd spit out the Gerber Ravioli and suck down the carrot chunks as if they were candy. Strangest kid I'd ever seen."

But tonight I wasn't there for the food. Angel was going to be there according to Emerson. Rumor had it that Angel was possibly planning on making the move permanent if he could find work. I was hoping to add to that incentive but by 8 p.m. he still hadn't shown up. Large groups of crowds never really appealed to me, maybe because during my father's long career as a politician we never seemed to get a moment alone in private.

He thrived on the attention but I usually avoided it if I could. So tonight I found my way out of the sliding glass door and onto the back wooden deck. It was a nice house. Emerson had done well to find one on the beach, but made even better by the fact that it was somewhat isolated. Well, as isolated as beachfront property can be anyway.

The sun had set on what had been a warm day, bringing a cool breeze as the first of the lustrous stars began to reflect the beauty of our Maker above.

I sat there reflecting, alone on the porch swing, rocking to the sound of the ocean, massaged by the calm crashing of the waves on the beach.

"Clear your mind," the old lady had said to me first thing every Tuesday afternoon that I laid out on her sticky leather couch.

"So how are you sleeping?" she'd ask.

It was always the same answer, "I'm not."

Sleep had become a relative term to me in recent years. They were more like catnaps in between nightmares. Always the same dream.

"Tell me," she'd prod.

Well, *Dr.* it's the same as last time."

"Still, I want to hear it," she'd encourage.

"Well, there I was again, tied up in the darkness of the warehouse. I can hear them arguing amongst themselves in the other room. One of them wants to move me to another spot, the other keeps saying 'Stick to the plan.' So again, I've just about freed my right arm from the restraint and I hear someone cussing and swearing just outside the window. But it's not an angry tone, it's more like whoever it is has stubbed their toe or something." I paused to consider this, if it was really Angel that day. I'd have to ask what had caused the outburst.

"Please continue." She'd prod again.

"Ok, so um, then I hear it….."

"The window again?" She always pretended to be interested at this point.

"Yes, the window." I'd say, as she leaned forward in her chair, saying, "Remember how I told you that dreams are all symbolic. The 'window' represents a new way of looking at life. This is the moment in your dream where you recognize a change is in the offing. So continue, please."

"Ok, so anyway, I hear the window open and then this loud thump as he enters the room. I don't know why, but somehow I find this humorous."

"How does he make you feel?" she'd ask calmly.

"Safe, warm."

"But we agreed that he is not real, correct?"

"Yes." Every time I lied like that, I'd feel as though I were betraying him.

"Angel is your conscience awareness. He is the strong side of Casey that is funny and brave and makes light of the situation. He is the father you always wanted, the mother to tuck you in, the friend to laugh with. But he is not real. He is you. Do you understand?"

"Yes." Guilt.

"Ok. So continue."

She'd pretend to take notes on her little notepad. But once while she was in the restroom I sneaked a peek. Circles. Nothing but endless circles going round and round. She'd come back from her break and sit down not noticing her pad had been moved, looking up at me as if I were the cause of the delay. Taking the cue, I'd drone on.

It was always the same story. I'd be freed and brought back home safe and sound. The only difference being his face. It was never a ski mask in my dreams. Once he was a 4 foot tall Chinaman complete with Fu-Manchu white beard and Asian accent. Next, he was a seven foot tall German wrestler complete with lederhosen and wooden shoes.

Each time her explanation was somewhat different, but the fact that Angel was not real was how it always ended. Then she would try to convince me to "just try hypnosis, just once," but no can do. She was licensed to practice her craft, but not to enter my mind and do what she will. She was steeped in eastern philosophies and ideas which included a form of meditation requiring one to 'clear the mind of all thought.'

The exact opposite in fact of what the Bible teaches, which says that one should 'meditate on things you had learned.' Meaning to learn from principles and past examples. But it definitely does not mean to vacate your thinking faculties. Besides, I once learned from a book on reasoning that "humans by nature have limitations. Additionally, their experience in life is relatively brief and is usually confined to one culture or environment. The knowledge they possess is thus restricted and everything is interconnected to such an extent that they constantly find aspects that they had not adequately considered. Any philosophy that they originate will reflect these limitations."

So it went with my psychiatrist. I basically picked and chose what to accept from our sessions. But one thing was for sure. She'd never convince me that he didn't exist. I knew him to be real and if that much, my touch with reality was really lost, well then I had lost more than just my friend Angel. I had lost myself. Which apparently I had been doing for those last few moments sitting on that deck.

I don't know how long he'd been standing there, only that he came from the direction of the beach.

"You wanna get outta here?" he asked, standing partially hidden in the shadows of the palm trees.

This wasn't the clumsy cashier. His dark eyes and daring posture gave him somewhat of an ominous look. He was confident, there was no mistaking that. But also he seemed more sure of his surroundings, his presence, as though he belonged to the nighttime hours. Moving closer, seemingly without a sound, he held out his hand. I didn't answer him audibly, though there was much said inside, rather I stepped off of the porch and laid my hand in his. I don't know why, but his touch felt like *home* to me. He led me down the beach, quietly, circling back to the street level. Once in the parking lot, he opened the door for me as we got into his truck. Careful Casey, ever the gentleman but still, he's dangerous.

To say I was nervous is an epic understatement. I think I said something like. "You know run flats are only good for about fifty miles."

"What?" he said, perplexed.

"You still don't have a spare on the back," I explained.

"Oh."

"Angel?" I ventured further.

"Yes?" he answered. And with such a small word, years of confusion and sometimes hope, came to rest in my heart, still …..

"This is the same Jeep, isn't it? The one you used back near Mexico."

"Clever girl ….. Micah."

"What?" I asked, leading. Hoping he'd fill in the blanks.

"My name is Micah. *Angel* is my daughter's name, sorry about the confusion"

"Ok. But before we go down this road together, and I have lots of questions obviously, I'd feel more comfortable if we weren't all alone. You know, it's best to be cautious, all things considered."

"Oh, we're not alone. I'm using my latest invention – E-CHAPERONE." he said proudly, lightening up a bit.

"E what?"

"E-CHAPERONE. It's a service I came up with wherein the entire date is filmed via this mini camera," he said, displaying a small button sized camera on his lapel. "So," he continued, "you can feel free to say Hi to Emerson anytime you want." He smiled, pleased with himself.

"Hi Mike," I queried.

"Hi Casey!" Mike's voice came booming over the stereo speakers.

"So this is a *date*?" I asked.

"What else?" he said, as though stating the obvious.

"Well, don't remember being asked is all."

"Funny ….. I thought I did." He said, pausing, waiting no doubt to see if I'd agree.

"When?" I teased.

"Uh, when I said 'You wanna get outta here?" he chuckled.

I was beating around the bush though, as I knew the questions I wanted to ask.

"Truth?" I asked gingerly, attempting to cross the divide.

"Truth," he acquiesced.

"Who are you really and how did you find me? And why didn't you simply come out and tell me who you were?" I asked, resisting the tears that began to sting the corners of my eyes. "Do you realize," I continued, getting louder and losing the battle with my emotions, "Do you realize that I went through years, YEARS! of therapy, thinking I was out of my mind?! And that a simple 'hello' from you could've saved me countless hardships and pain? Do you know how crazy you made me look? How foolish I've seemed to my friends, my dad, even myself? The tears began to flow as I exercised what was left of the years of restraint. Then, breathless, I just floundered there, exhausted and spent, silent. We rode along like that, quietly, as he waited for a sign I was about done. But I was far from done, still, I gave him a moment.

"I'm sorry. Though I know those words do not begin to cover the harm I have caused, still it must be said, and I've waited far too long to say it, so first, I'm sorry. Second, it wasn't possible for me to reveal all to you until just recently on account of the fact that I am an ex-convict who until just this last year, was waist deep in a custody battle over my daughter. The judge had specifically warned me to stay away from other ex-convicts and there was no way to explain it, had the word of that initial rescue gotten out.

"Well, how do you explain it Micah? How do you explain knowing where I was on that night?" I asked, half of me not wanting to hear the answer.

"I had known of the kidnappers plans to take you, as they had originally expected me to participate. At first I thought that they wouldn't follow through, but once the news broke of your abduction, I knew I had to do something. There's this scripture in Deuteronomy 24:

7 that speaks of the penalties for kidnapping. I felt that because I knew of the plan, I owed it to you to break it up. But if I went to the police, it was possible that the kidnappers would've heard the call over their scanners and in a panic, killed you. I couldn't risk that. After we were free I could've at that point told you who I was, but then there was the media everywhere and I knew you'd be interrogated. Couldn't chance losing my daughter over my involvement with it."

"So what about the garage incident, how'd you find me there, and who were you fighting with?"

"The knife. It was one of my first inventions, I'd made it to track my daughter Angel, thus the code name Angel."

I pulled it out of my purse, turning it over in my hands. That of course made perfect sense to me. That's why he'd panicked when Ron was using it as a crow bar. I opened it, and as I did, his phone rang. He pulled it out before me revealing a lit up screen.

'ANGEL ….. ANGEL."

"You see," he pointed, taking it from me, "it's also got a tracking device," he explained, as I now heard him in double, his voice echoing through the phone speakers.

"Yak, to your second question," he said solemnly, changing to a more serious tone.

"Who?" I asked, sensing his trepidation.

"Maniac Yak. Couldn't let him get a hold of you, and I was doing quite well until you bopped me over the head, *thank you very much*," he said with a smile, rubbing his head.

"So all of this was out of a sense of moral duty? Is that what you're telling me? That's the only reason you did it?"

He turned to look at me as he pulled the truck up to the cliff's edge. I hadn't even noticed how far we'd driven or where we even were. But when he opened the door for me, I found myself inches from the edge of a vast canyon stretching out below. It was a panoramic view of the entire city, lit up by the stars that canvassed the night. I had never seen such a beautiful sight.

He took my hand while moving behind me, eventually wrapping his arms around me. I stood there in silence, my doubts collapsing in his embrace. I could've stayed there all night, listening to the air waft up the canyon wall, the rhythm of his heart so close as he leaned in, whispering "not the only reason."

CHAPTER 22

DATING CASEY

He'd wanted to say more that night. Much more. But the battle in his mind told him that some things were better left unsaid.

He'd already lost Angel. She'd hardly spent any time at all with him that summer, withdrawing herself emotionally, and now she wanted to go back home as she missed her 'boyfriend' back in Seattle. So that gave Casey and him a week to get to know one another.

The week passed by faster than he'd have liked, with the two of them spending nearly every waking moment together. She'd loved the trip to Sea World on Friday. They couldn't seem to stop smiling after coming out of the dolphin's tank. He'd often dreamed of what it would be like in a paradise where the animals were at peace with humans. And although Sea World wasn't quite paradise, still, being with her it seemed close enough. It wasn't long before she began to anticipate him, his needs, and subtle moods. Moving in unison as though they'd somehow always known each other. The way she smiled so easily when something went wrong. It drove him crazy and yet, drew him to her even more while he desperately tried to fix the universe. Always uneasy with loose ends and unfinished business. Yet it didn't seem to bother her. She seemed to know he needed to do it.

Once during a family study, she burst into a giggle fit when he'd tried to explain, "There's a scripture that says, 'the stupid one is folding his hands and is eating his own flesh.'" He had no idea why it was so funny to her, but it took only a few more moments before they were both laughing uncontrollably.

That was what he loved about her. She had a way of letting things go with a shrug, while assuring him it'd be ok if he just let it go. Course he never did. Yet, she had profound respect for him that he could readily sense. Sometimes it was the way in which she listened to him, as though he was the only person in the world that knew something on that subject. And then there were the times, far too many times in his opinion, when he'd say something rash without thinking it through. She'd just wait there silently, looking at him with those sympathetic eyes, knowing an apology or further explanation was coming. It was that 'benefit of the doubt' he'd never gotten from anyone else other than Emerson. Emerson had known him for years, had seen him in action, thus it was no surprise that he'd grown that kind of trust. But she was different. Her respect seemed instinctive, natural. She didn't just 'believe' he wouldn't hurt her. She knew he wouldn't. In a world full of uncertainty, he was now absolutely sure of just two things. He had the right religion and he had the right girl. He couldn't afford to lose track of her again. And he knew there was just one way of achieving that.

CHAPTER 23

CASEY'S DIARY
ENTRY 402

Dear diary,

    Admittedly my entries are becoming fewer and farther in between. But this is a good thing diary. I have him now to talk to, to relate to. Ok, so he's not as great a listener as you. Ha, ha. But he does listen, I mean really listens. He even hears what I don't say. I feel like I really know him. What he is inside. I know his eyes in the morning sun. The light strands of brown that color them 'hermoso.' A word I learned from him that in Spanish means 'beautiful.' You see diary, he's even gotten me speaking in tongues. Except it's not Holy Spirit that I'm filled with when I speak it.

    I woke up and looked in the mirror this morning. Why is it when I see him I'm intentionally blind to his flaws, but when I look at myself, flaws is all I see?

    When he left for Seattle this morning, he had to literally tear himself out of my arms. I asked him not to forget me. He smiled and said, "How could I forget you? Aside from Emerson, you're the only one I know." It was such a funny and yet true statement. In our time together his phone never rang. Other than Emerson, he seemed to have no close acquaintances. Strange because he is quite intelligent and charming. Yet it appears that he has let very few people in. Most likely the result of 'childhood trauma' the old lady would've said.

In my life I've had many relationships, most of which were dysfunctional, with friends, relatives, even boyfriends. They all had one thing in common. I felt drained at the end of the day. Micah is the opposite. I'm recharged continually in his presence. Much like a candle that loses nothing by lighting another candle.

Diary, I wanna keep him. It's the possibility of having a dream come true that makes life interesting, right? He's going to be gone for a week now and I keep worrying that he won't come back, that he'll disappear once again. But as Micah once said, "Don't worry darling. Worry is the interest you pay on trouble before it is due." Still I worried right up until I got the mail today. Clever as he is, he must've mailed it before he left. It read:

A SONG FOR MY DARLING CASEY
"NOT ALONE"

I WISH THAT I COULD GIVE YOU EVERYTHING
YOU NEED EVERYTHING YOU WANT
EVERYTHING YOU PRAY FOR
WHEN YOU THINK NO ONE'S LISTENING TO YOUR
PRAYERS IN THE DARK
I WISH THAT I COULD GIVE YOU EVERYTHING
YOU DREAMED IN THAT SONG YOU WROTE
THAT YOU SING TO YOURSELF WHEN YOU THINK
NO ONE'S LISTENING IN THE DARK
AND EVEN THOUGH YOU'RE FEELING SO ALONE
YOU'RE NOT
AND EVEN THOUGH IT SEEMS LIKE HOPE IS
GONE, IT'S NOT
CAUSE I WILL HELP YOU PRAY AND
I WILL HELP YOU SING AND
I WILL HELP YOUR DREAMS
REALITY
AND I WILL HELP YOU PRAY AND
I WILL HELP YOU SING AND
I WILL HELP YOU DREAM
REALITY

CHAPTER 24

"OUT OF THE HEART"

The trip to Seattle had been arduous, Micah thought as he arrived back in California after a week best left forgotten in his opinion.

It had all started out with the long drive up I-5 with his daughter. A moment alone that he'd thought he had been longing for. However, as she began to explain her future plans (which he couldn't convince her out of) it became painfully obvious that she would have to learn from the most unforgiving teacher, experience.

In chilling detail she went on to explain how she was going to get her ears gauged. A process in which her lobes would be expanded in gruesome lengths.

He'd asked what she'd planned to do for a living looking that way. "Dad, everyone has things like this done these days," she'd declared righteously, rolling her eyes. He had yet to meet 'everyone' but was fairly sure it didn't include him.

That conversation, among many, had been playing over and over in his head like a broken record. He reflectively tugged on an ear lobe and smiled, hearing Casey's voice in his head, 'let it go babe, just let it go.'

Upon entering town, Emerson let him know that Casey was rock climbing with some friends up in Rattle Snake Canyon. Rock climbing was her favorite outdoor activity and she was no slouch at it. His first lesson had him rappelling a fifty foot sheer cliff face. Terrified wasn't quite the way to describe his sentiments, but it was close.

Yet she was unencumbered dangling from a rope at great heights.

He got his first glimpse of her as he rounded a corner in the Canyon Valley early Saturday morning. She was halfway up a rock face nearly sixty yards off the ground with another twenty or so to reach the top. He could just make it there if he hurried. "Driving to the top would be cheating" she'd scolded him when she'd given him his first lesson on that very same outcropping. But this time he was hoping she would be pleasantly surprised as he had driven all night in order to show up a day early.

Just as he'd hoped, he arrived just as the tips of her fingers gripped the top of the ledge. She stood up, and seeing him, all but toppled backward before he arrested her fall with a firm hand, embracing her into a hug.

"Do you remember when you first brought me here, and as I hesitated you asked me what I was most afraid of?"

"Yes ….. yes," she stuttered, clenching him tightly as though he might fly away.

"Well. I'm afraid of not being able to come to your aid when you need me most, like when you sprained your ankle back in Seattle. I'm afraid of being trapped somehow where I can't come to you. I'm afraid of handcuffs," he said resolutely.

"*Handcuffs?*" she mused, puzzled.

"There are many ways a man can be handcuffed. Handcuffed physically so that I can no longer hold you. Handcuffed mentally from willful ignorance, as so many are. Handcuffed spiritually from lack of obedience. Handcuffed of heart from lack of humility. So ….. I'm afraid of handcuffs.

"Handcuffs," she repeated, mulling it over.

"But do you know what I am the most afraid of?" he invited.

"Um, I'm almost afraid to ask," she replied tentatively.

"I'm afraid of living the rest of my years having never had the courage to ask you to marry me," he said as he knelt before her.

It had taken two private detectives, countless medical records and in the end, an ordinary street vendor to find the perfect ring for her. But as she stood trembling before him, it appeared to have paid off.

"Hermoso," she stammered, taking it and sliding it on.

"It's your mother's," he said, disclosing his latest mission.

"What?! How did you find her?" she demanded.

"Uh, excuse me? Aren't you forgetting *something*?"

"What?" she teased.

"You didn't say 'yes' ….. or ….. 'no' for that matter."

"Funny, I thought I did," she chuckled.

"When?" he challenged.

"Do you really want to know?" she tortured, keeping him in suspense.

He nodded silently, bracing for the worst.

"I answer that question Micah, first thing every morning, before each and every meal, and just before I close my eyes at night ….. Yes, my Angel Micah ….. it has always been yes."

CHAPTER 25

CASEY'S DIARY
ENTRY 'LAST?'

Dear diary,

This may be my very last entry. No, it's not bad news.

Tomorrow I will be Mrs. Micah Tate. Wow, it just rolls right off the tongue so easily. Casey Sheila Tate. I'll have to get used to signing that. 'Fairy tales do come true' is the first line to my favorite song 'Young at Heart.' And for me, a fairy tale really is coming true. He's everything I've ever wanted and was sometimes too afraid to ask for. And as if things couldn't get any better, he's found mom. She will be at the wedding.

You hear all these stories of 'Bridezilla.' Brides that fight and fuss over every little detail, trying to create the perfect moment. But for me, if he just shows up, it'll be my definition of perfect.

Ok, ok, I am freaking out just a little bit over the flowers. But I am the florist, so you gotta give me that. Problem is, one of the main floral delivery trucks has, almost predictably, come up missing tonight, the night before the wedding. Still, love isn't about flowers that are here today and gone tomorrow. Love endures all, hopes all, believes all. Love never fails. And I am completely, unconditionally, in love with this man.

So perhaps this is goodbye diary. Maybe the next time you'll be opened up, it'll be in the hands of our someday to be daughter, Angelica.

Philia, Casey Tate

CHAPTER 26

WEDDING BELLS

The Santa Barbara County Courthouse was like something out of a Castilian dream. Replete with castle buttresses and ramparts. The courtyard boasted renaissance fountains and high vaulted porticoes over cobbled paths which wound their way around palm trees and manicured lawns.

But all of it paled in comparison to Casey, whose fire red hair and emerald eyes painted her like an angelic apparition to him.

"Micah, do you promise to keep and to love her so long as you both shall live, which hopefully will be a very long time?" the minister asked, elbowing him.

"I do." He answered solemnly.

"And do you Casey take Micah to be your lawfully wedded husband to love and to respect as long as you both shall live? Hopefully a very long time?" he continued.

Casey turned to Micah, pausing, peering deep into his eyes as though there was something ….. something else. And suddenly there wasn't anyone else around but the two of them, as his heart began to beat out of his chest while he waited nervously for her answer.

"Promise me, no matter what happens to us, you will always come back to me?" she asked genuinely, silencing the low buzz of the crowd.

"I will never leave you," he answered, taking her hand. I will always be nearby. Yes. I promise."

"In that case ……. I do."

CHAPTER 27

YAK'S REVENGE

Dry. Micah's throat was so dry. There was something wrong with his right eye and intense pain shot through his chest each time he took in a deep breath.

The room was pitch black, but large, judging from the cavernous sound. He could barely make out the faint sounds of traffic passing by some distance away.

He was handcuffed and shackled to a steel frame of some type that creaked and moaned as he wrangled with the restraints. The smell of decay and ash filled the air. His tongue tasted of iron and blood mixed with gear oil from whatever was left of his motorcycle.

He tried screaming out Casey's name for what must have been an hour or so. But despairingly, it met with no response as the agony of each strained breath brought him continually to the brink of blacking out.

Think Micah, think, he chided himself. What happened? Ok, the last he remembered they were riding the back roads of Canyon Valley to the lookout view. The place from their first date. That was immediately after the ceremony, as he had intended on showing her the new home he'd purchased just twenty miles from the bottom of the canyon. What had happened Micah? Think. We were riding my Ninja (an idea she had resisted because of the dress) and we came around a corner to an intersection …… Oh God!!! He hadn't seen the van coming until they had already passed the halfway point of the crossing. He had the green, didn't he? Yes, it was his light, but the van, the floral van, t-boned them with such force that it was clear that whomever the driver was hadn't even so much as pumped the brakes before the impact. And now it was difficult even to say what day it was, if it was in fact daytime at all.

"Casey!!!" he tried again, desperately.

'Ok, think Micah. What exactly did happen? Did you see a face in the windshield? No. It had happened too quickly. Were we being followed? Yes. YES.' He'd had the sensation of being followed for the last week or so but had excused it as pre-wedding jitters. Funny how love can disarm even the most cautious of creatures. Maybe that's why hunters find their prey so much easier in the spring time when the animals are pre-occupied with courtship.

When exactly did the paranoia begin? Hmmm. Back in Seattle when he'd found her mother's house.

There had been someone watching the house, he'd been sure of it at the time. Who was it? Who'd be …..

"YAK!!! Come on out! I know it's you!" Micah bellowed into the darkness.

"Monin Boss. Comfy? Cozy? His booming deep voice threw itself off of the walls, echoing.

"Yak, let's just leave her outta this, ok?" he begged, wrenching on his restraints.

"Them der is made of good half inch chain boss. Ain't no knife gonna cut you way this time," his voice came from all directions as Yak stalked Micah, circling him in the darkness.

"Yak, listen to me. This girl wasn't meant for you, just let her go."

"Ya no what Boss? Yall should be thankin me. If it wadn't for my quick thinking she might be dead by now, but I done saved her," he said innocently.

"Well if you saved her like you claim, then where is she Yak?" He compromised, trying to get Yak to divulge more information.

"She roun, don you worry," Yak replied, reveling in the moment.

"Yak, I swear to God, you will pay if you've hurt her!!!"

"Hurt her? Now why you gone and said something like that? Uh? Why would I hurt my own momma? You mus think I'm the one gone and bumped my head."

"Your mother? What are you talking about Yak, your mother's dead."

"SHE AIN'T DEAD!!!" he screamed, slapping Micah across the face. He didn't even see it coming. One thing was for sure Yak was in full control and Micah needed to come up with an alternate plan if they were to survive.

Remembering his lessons in psychology, there'd been a lesson on "Humanization." A concept that taught that if you spoke of personal things, such as family, parents, children, then you'd become more 'human' to the kidnapper. Making it more difficult for him to kill you.

"I know Yak," Micah continued on in a sympathetic tone, "I know she's alive in God's eyes."

"No!!!!!! She alive right now!!!" he declared.

"How Yak? Didn't you say she'd died giving birth to you?"

"Yeah. Sho you right. She died, but daddy told me her last word was that she'd wished she could've seen me as an adult. And I know how all things come round eventually. See now. It was FATE. When I first saw momma, I knew it was her. That look in her eyes, well, it just stilled my heart and stopped time. And I know, just as good as I am live, that she's my true momma, just re-incarnated."

"Who Yak?"

"CASEY, YOU FOO! She my ma. An you ain't gonna take her from me dis time. No matta what!"

"Yak," Micah reasoned, "the Bible says ….."

"Shut up!!! You just go on head an shut up now! I done heard nuff of you Biba thumpers! See now, that's what yall fail to understand. We all existed before. All of us was once someone else. Everything repeats itself in history. Fact, what I'm bout to do has already been done. Now that there's a fact! Ya know, truth is, I feel sorry for all yall Biba thumpers walkin round in darkness, just like you is right now. Sin. Ha! What is sin? I tell what sin is….. sin is a man-made concept, contrived by the greedy to scare yall into puttin money in that box. Isn't that right?"

"Well ……" Micah tried.

"Shut up!" He struck him again, this time from somewhere behind. "You shut up naw! I ain't gonna tell you gin. Now, where was I? Oh, yeah. Sin. Ha. Guilt. Doubba ha! Guilty for what? Huh? For thangs that was gonna happen anyway? Now I done tried to be nice. I done tried it yo way. I prayed. You don thank I done tried to pray before?" he demanded, becoming more agitated.

"No, I know you pray Yak," Micah responded calmly. "DON'T YOU PATRONIZE ME!!! I know what you think of me! Yall think I'm stupid. Yeah I know. But I'm not the one tied up, now am I? Tell me somthin Biba thumpa, where your God na? Huh? Cat got yo tongue? Go ahead, you call him, I'll wait. I got plenty time. No? I ain't seein no kinda angels to save ya. What happen? See I'm tryin to help you now. But you don want no help, do ya. Do you know what natural selection is Boss?"

"I've heard of it." Micah replied firmly, finally tiring of the rant.

"Yeah. You didn't think I known bout that na, huh? Natural selection Boss ….. is where people like you who refuse to learn, get wiped out! Extinct! Just like the dinosaurs."

"Where's Casey, Yak?" Micah pleaded, fear rising in his voice.

"Where Casey ….. where Casey?" Yak repeated in mock imitation. "Pitifa! You know that Boss? You disgust me. Where da old Boss at? Huh? What happen to the guy I knows in prison? Yall could've been part of something so special. So pure. A family. Don't you wan a family Boss?" he asked, while Micah tried to get a fix on his location in the darkness.

"Yes Yak. I want a family. More than anything." And it was true, he thought to himself.

"Well na. That more like it! Mom, you hear that? He wan a family. You can come out na."

Suddenly the lights were turned on, blinding him, as Micah's eyes struggled to adjust.

"Casey?" he ventured.

She stood before him, just at the foot of the bed frame, dressed in an apron and knitted shawl. She wore makeup, smeared on, like that of an eighty-year old woman would wear, slightly off center. A silver gray wig sat haphazardly atop her head as a small line of blood marked her cheek from where it had run down from her ear. She was shaking uncontrollably as she stood there holding a breakfast in a bed tray before him, like a waitress at a macabre wax museum.

"You hungry Boss?" Yak stepped out from behind him, dangling a charred rat by its tail. That accounted for the ashy smell of decomposition, he thought. Casey must have just been dying there holding that tray of charred meat, her being a vegetarian and all. His sympathy must've been readable as Yak looked at his own helping.

"What? Rat aint good enough for ya Boss? And I thought you'd have no problem eatin one of your own." Yak snarled.

"What are you talking about?" Micah dared to ask.

"You! You're a RAT! You done ratted out yo own friends! Don't you go lying to me na. I knowz it wad you called them police in Oregon."

Micah said nothing, his eyes now fully adjusted. He tried to conceal the shocked look on his face as he realized what he saw before him was not out of focus, but rather, very real. Yak was barely recognizable. Night vision goggles hung from around his neck, but what had arrested his attention was Yak's face. The right side appeared to have decayed to such an extent, that everything from his eye to his jaw appeared to be melting. The gash on his cheek was open and liquefying with pus. Clearly he hadn't sought out any medical attention after the incident on Hill Top.

"Shocked Boss? Yeah I was surprised too. You'd think your ole boss Bajwa wouda paid for a real alarm system for that store. Ha! But you remember whenst you told me that before yall go and break a door down, check da handles first? Well dat ole man didn't have no security system. Ha! Dem signs was fake!" Yak began to laugh, as he showed off his goggles. "Tell you what. I don't know how yall worked for that cheap man so many year, but I done paid him back" he boasted.

"What did you do to Bajwa, Yak?" Micah interrogated, as though he were still somehow in control.

"Lax Boss. I just stole the goggles and a few a dem speakers. Yall know dat white boy Ronnie can rap? I bet he a big star one day."

Casey stood there silently at the foot of the bed with a look of deep concern on her face. He was worried for her, but he could see by the worried expression on her face that she was far more worried about him. He must look worse than he feels, he thought.

He looked her over closely, trying to sit up. Her ankle was shackled to the bed also and there appeared to be some bruising around the cuff. She lifted up the leg slightly for him while following his gaze. Good girl, he thought. Already aware that he was in the planning process.

To that end, he also took in the contours of the warehouse with a critical eye. Trying to discern the weak spots and windows. Surely he'd locked the doors. Regardless of his own advice of trying the handle.

The warehouse was nearly empty. It appeared to be an old print shop, long since abandoned with the wireless boom. Scattered sheets of paper rustled about on the floor. Two main loading dock doors dominated the room, framing the far wall. Both were securely locked with a chain at the center. Three or four offices dotted the corners but for the most part it appeared that the three of them were the only ones in the factory. That is except for the large floral van parked just inside, sporting a newly caved in front end.

Micah shuddered when he thought of the impact.

Looking Casey over again, more intently now as she seemed to be calming down a bit. Her eyes wandered in concern for his wounded eye, then back to his bandaged face. Noticing their silent communication, Yak interrupted.

"Oh. Your eye Boss? Is that what you worried about? Yall worry too much. Ha! Mama been beggin me for two days to bring you to the hospital but I told her you be just fine."

Micah looked at Casey with the expression, 'two days?' as she discreetly nodded 'Yes.'

"Yeah," Yak continued, "Them hospitals aint good fa nuttin you ask me. Ha. Mo people dying in dem hospitals than anywhere else. How you explain that? Mean, look at me. I aint never been to a hospital and I'm just fine. Still mama nagged and nagged me till finally I let her put dem bandages on ya. You know how ma is," he concluded triumphantly, as though they were all on the same team.

"Yeah, I know how she is." Micah teased her, trying to bring some levity to the situation. She glared back, crinkling her nose with a smirk.

"Yeah, I knowz you know, cuz you done gone and married her, huh?" Yak asked, trying to make sense of his own twisted logic. "Ya know," he continued, "when I'd said 'no' the first time, she done tried to cut me wid this thang," he exclaimed, pulling out the butterfly knife from his pocket.

That seemed to get Casey's attention, as she looked at Micah, eyes opening wide. Yak began swiveling the knife open and shut, trying to get the hang of it.

"Ow!!!" he yelped, as the blade dug out a chunk of his skin. "I don't know how yall do this thang! Toys like dis here oughtta be kept way from children. Right mom?" he asked, seeking her approval.

"Right" Casey said with authority. "Now you open that knife up and lock it son. Then you just put it back on that table over there." She demanded.

"Why would I want to do that ma?" Yak asked childishly.

"You don't argue with your mother son! Now do what I say." Casey played the role well, Micah thought. It was almost scary how she could get into a role.

Yak reluctantly did as he was told, as Casey stood over him, hands on her hips.

"You see now, Boss? yall had it all wrong. Stealin cars from common folk. Na me? I steal em from companies, cuz they got so many it'd be a week before they done knowd it's gone." Yak was now on a roll. Clearly in his element. Unquestionably, Micah thought, he had underestimated Yak by thinking he was mentally challenged. It was now becoming very clear to him that Yak was in fact, pre-planning things in advance. He wasn't simply reacting on raw emotion. No, Yak was intentional in his efforts. Deliberate in his movements. No doubt, in all the premeditation, he'd thought out an end plan for his game. A plan that included Casey only. Micah would have to be dealt with soon. This didn't bode well.

'Son. It's bed time. Now you go on and take a nap. I need to feed your brother." She ordered, as though this routine had gone on for days. Yak bowed his head as though he were a petulant child rebuked by a teacher. But he obeyed all the same, slouching his massive shoulders and turning to leave.

"Well," he pouted, "I'm going to sleep, but yall better not try to escape. We family na, and the soon ya'll figure that out the betta yall gonna be." Climbing the stairs leading to a side office, he took one last look, and satisfied, closed the door.

"Are you ok?" she asked, taking off the wig.

"I'm ok. Did, did he ….. ?" he asked reluctantly.

"No. He didn't ….. I look terrible, don't I?" She asked, trying to smear the makeup off.

It was the first time he really noticed that she was still wearing her wedding dress, torn up though it was. It was barely recognizable, as it was anything but white. Still, her sharp green eyes and loving smile overshadowed the 'I just survived a hurricane' look she was sporting.

"You're beautiful ….. you've always been beautiful to me" he answered cautiously, reaching out and taking her hand. "How do I look?" he countered.

"Like you were run over by a truck," she chuckled, cracking an enormous smile, lighting up her face.

"Hey, what's with the brutal honesty?"

"What? My husband doesn't like it *rough*? She said, jumping up onto the bed, straddling him. Her chain noisily dragged along the ground behind her, reminding him that although this had been somewhat of a secret fantasy of his, still ..... better times could be found for it. "You know what?" she asked playfully, bouncing up and down.

"I'm almost afraid to ask?" he teased, though this time with an undertone of seriousness.

"I still have a *wedding* gift for you. Oh, I was planning on waiting until our first night together but ...." she paused. "I guess now is as good a time as any," she said as she reached into her bra.

"Wait a minute! Wait a minute darling! Hold on now ......" he exclaimed, reaching to stop her hands.

"What? Oh ..... no .... I mean yes ....but ..... no, that wasn't the wedding gift. Well I guess yes, so yes I have that gift too, but your first gift was to be this," she said as she reached in and pulled out a small golden handcuff key dangling from the end of a platinum chain.

"What? Where did you ....?" He mumbled, taking it and bringing it close to his good eye. "Does it ......?"

"Work? Yes. It's a real Highway Patrol handcuff key, plated in gold of course," She beamed proudly.

"So, you mean you could've escaped at any time?" he asked, surprised.

"For better or worse," she countered. "Besides, this thing only unlocks your cuffs, but this" ...... she lifted up her ankle for him to inspect. The dilemma became obvious.

Yak was smart. The shackle that each of them had been wearing was an antique of some sort. Possibly from way back in the slave trade days. Really, it was nothing more than a thick, rusty iron U-shaped bolt, with a bar lock sealing both ends around the ankle and two large nuts to lock the plate in place. No key. He examined it closely as she explained, "I watched him screw these on both of us. He actually screwed them on with his bare hands. I tried several times to unscrew it myself, but apparently he is very, very strong."

"I know," Micah replied solemnly. "Too bad we don't have WD-40, I'll bet those nuts would slide right off," he concluded, while attempting to unscrew the first nut unsuccessfully.

"We do," she said, leaning down, laying on his chest.

"Darling? You care to explain that last statement?" he asked, kissing her forehead.

"You know ….." she teased, "he's going to be asleep for at least an hour or so …….."

"Darling ….."

"Ok, ok ….. when we were loading you up in the truck I noticed the can of WD-40 lying in the road. It came from your bike's storage compartment, I assume."

He nodded, urging her to continue.

"Well, I grabbed it and got in the van, thinking maybe I could use it for a type of mace or something if I got a chance later." She finished, as though there were no need to explain further.

"So what you're saying is …." He asked, trying to make sense of it all. "What you're saying is, that I was knocked out and you were free to run, but you somehow willfully got into the van with him? Am I saying this right?" he asked incredulously.

"Not exactly," she corrected. "I was trying to drag you away from the wreck as Yak was getting out of the van. I realized that I had a chance to run but Yak offered me a deal. He told me that if I came willingly, we could get you some help. But if I ran, he would kill you where you lay. As it was impossible to outrun him while dragging you behind, I got in the van. Had to. Then he dragged you inside with us. We drove here then we waited for you to wake up. You were starting to scare me for a while there, but I just kept thinking of your promise to me."

"Promise?"

"That you'd always come back to me," she said, caressing his cheek. "Anyway, it's not as bad as it looks."

"What, my face?"

"No, the rat. I had some, it's not as bad as it looks," she chuckled, dismounting.

"Funny," he smiled. "Glad you're having fun here, but can we get down to business?" he said sternly. Reading his eyes she nodded in agreement, knowing playtime was over.

"What do you wanna do love? We're both shackled to this bed."

"Well ….." he said, getting up as she un-handcuffed his hands from the frame. "Let's pick the bed up and move it over to the van to get the WD-40. Unless you have a better idea."

They worked well together as a team. The two of them surrounded the bed frame and began to lift as it creaked in protest. But a few steps into the trip she began another giggle fit, annoying him.

"What's so funny Casey?"

"Well ...... grumpy pants, this is how we first met ….." she answered nostalgically, trying to hold back the laughter. Pausing for a moment, Micah tried not to look at her face, knowing the urgency. But ultimately it didn't work. A meeting of the eyes was all it took before he too lost the battle and began laughing cautiously, trying not to wake Yak. But the more they tried to keep it quiet, the funnier it got. It was a relief to both of them when they finally reached the van.

Inside he discovered a catastrophic wonderland of rose petals strewn everywhere about the inner cabin. It took a few nervous moments before they located the spray can hidden under a floral bouquet.

Bringing the bed back to its original position, they settled into the work of spraying, turning, spraying and turning again and again torqueing on the bolts that seemed to protest against every rotation. Yet, slowly they began gaining ground due to Micah and Casey's combined efforts. Casey's bolt came loose first, but they decided to leave the last thread on until the last possible moment, just in case Yak returned before Micah could get free. In this way they figured, Yak wouldn't have reason for suspicion if he suddenly interrupted. Just as long as the shackles appeared to remain intact he wouldn't react rashly. Next, they set to work on Micah's shackle, finally taking it all the way off and preparing to loose hers and leave when .... "HEY!!!!!! WHAT IS GOING ON HERE?!!!" Yak suddenly appeared, apparently through an unseen back door.

Bursting into the room, he headed straight for Casey. Yanking her violently backwards by her still attached shackle, he dragged her screaming across the floor. Yak picked up the wig and harshly slammed it down on her head. "WHY CAN'T YOU PEOPLE PLAY NICE?!!! YOU THINK MICAH IS SOME KINDA HERO, DO YA?!!! HE'S WORSE THAN ME. HE HIDES BEHIND HIS BIBLE AND DOESN'T TELL YOU THE TRUTH, MOM!!! YOU THINK I'M THE BAD GUY, HUH? WELL ASK YOUR ANGEL THAT YOU LOVE SO MUCH ...... WHO PLANNED YOUR KIDNAPPING IN THE FIRST PLACE?!!! DO YOU EVEN REALIZE WHO IT WAS THAT PUT HIM IN PRISON? IT WAS YOUR DAD CASEY. HE HAS BEEN PLAYING

YOU ALL ALONG!!!" He screamed, scowling, as he drug her by the arm to the foot of the bed. "ASK HIM!!!" He demanded.

Casey stood there, silently, waiting for Micah to jump up out of the bed. Knowing that his leg was loose, although currently concealed under the blankets.

But the look Micah gave her, in response to the statement, caused her to tremble. Suddenly she was far more afraid now, facing Micah, than she had been with the entire situation at hand. Her brave disposition changed instantly, as she reluctantly asked. "Babe, what is he talking about?"

"WELL ANSWER HER!!!" Yak demanded, sensing an opening.

She deserved the answer, Micah thought to himself. He'd held that piece of information in his heart for far too long. "I planned it Casey. It was my idea," he admitted dejectedly.

Casey tilted her head, peering deep into his eyes, trying to determine if he was telling the truth. She waited there, hoping he had something to add but as the silence became deafening, she finally, seemingly having come to terms with it all, whispered under her breath, "No." then fainted, collapsing to the ground.

The room fell silent. Yak and Micah stared at each other across the divide, as though all of the years of cat and mouse had finally, thankfully, climaxed into that moment.

Notably, the passing traffic noise in the background seemed to be becoming louder and louder with each passing moment, until the both of them turned their attention to the big bay doors. Yak let go of Casey's chain and turned to investigate.

Micah, seeing his attention was distracted momentarily, reacted quickly, reaching down and unscrewing the last revolution of Casey's shackle, freeing her and grasping her limp body into his arms.

Yak paused, having reached the loading dock doors. A small gust of wind wafted up from under the doors, sweeping papers up with its current as the traffic noise crescendoed into a deafening roar.

"BOOOOM!!!!!!"

The entire wall came crashing inward with a violent implosion of glass blasting into the room, launching the van, the doors and Yak into the air with a cloud of dust and steel cycloning like an enraged demon.

The Santa Barbara City bus came rumbling to a stop frighteningly close, just feet from Casey and Micah.

The digital read out sign read, 'TRUTH.' Strange sign Micah thought, as the driver's side doors opened.

"Sorry I'm late," Emerson smiled.

"Well, it wouldn't be a city bus if it were on time I suppose," Micah quipped, as he carried the slowly waking Casey up the stairs. Emerson put it in reverse and slowly began backing out of the warehouse as though he were a professional bus driver looking for a spot to park.

"So," Micah asked, taking a seat, "What's with the sign?"

Emerson smiled broadly, looking in his rearview mirror while turning toward the highway. "Oh, that?" he asked innocently. "I thought you'd like it ...... you know, 'The *TRUTH* shall set you free'?"

CHAPTER 28

BUS RIDE TO NOWHERE

"How did you find us?" Micah asked as they rode through the canyon roads back to Santa Barbara.

"Well. The couch in my living room had been vibrating for a while I guess. I didn't notice it but apparently it was driving my dog crazy. When I went to investigate, I found the cell phone hidden between two cushions. I figured maybe you guys were playing around with the knife or something so I was going to ignore it altogether. Then I heard Yak's voice, though I didn't know it was him at the time. But what I did know was that you guys didn't show up at the new house in the valley. And that the screen on the cell phone was pointing to the old business district. So, I put two and two together," he concluded proudly.

Emerson seemed right at home behind the wheel of the large vehicle. Micah didn't need to ask how he came across it, as Emerson was widely known as the best mechanic in town. He could fix motorcycles, boat engines, and yes, even diesel bus engines. Emerson could be found about town, driving exotic cars and rare trucks. "The price you pay for good work," he'd always say.

Casey sat isolated at the far back of the bus having said, "I just need a few moments alone, please." It was the 'please' comment that bothered him. The two of them had grown so close that they rarely ever said please, knowing that everything they had they would share. But she had said 'please' as though those were her final words on the subject. She may have said, 'a *moment alone*,' but he knew her expressions well and what she'd actually said was for far longer than just a 'moment.'

Micah didn't know what to say to her anyway. What really could he say? Actions speak louder than words and ultimately planning her kidnapping was more like a scream. She had seen with her own eyes, both sides of him. The past and the present. The problem was, that the 'present' him had been holding back critical information, information that now had her sitting with her back to him. If this was the way he was going to lose her, he thought, then he wasn't really sure Emerson's rescue had really been a rescue at all.

Emerson had already radioed ahead, alerting the police and calling an ambulance for Yak. But as they had left, Yak was nowhere to be found among the wreckage and Micah had the distinct feeling that if the police didn't hurry Yak would get away again. Casey and Micah hadn't sustained any real damage in the collision. Well, physically anyway.

A profound sadness entered Micah's heart, eventually settling down deep in his stomach like a stone. It was as if he was being rejected by God at the final hour. Made worse by the fact that he fully knew he deserved it.

"Drop me off here Emerson," Micah said dejectedly after a while.

"What? I'm not going to drop you off here. We're in the middle of nowhere. Besides, the police are going to want your version of the story."

"What story would that be, Emerson? The story that I deceived the one and only woman I have ever loved? That I set up her kidnapping, introduced her to a madman psychopath and nearly got her killed? Oh, but I'm innocent, because now I'm a Jehovah's Witness, so please don't put me away for the rest of my life?" Micah posed sarcastically.

"Micah, you're my best friend. Listen to me. The truth will set you free."

"Free? Emerson? Really? Freedom? You think that's what I want? Why would I want that? Why do I deserve that? What good is freedom without love? Have I taught you nothing? Life is just a long line of the dead ones waiting for eternal sleep, without love."

"She'll come around," he replied. "You'll see. They always come around."

"THEY do not apply to her and I. Now LET ME OUT!!!" he demanded.

Pulling off to the side of the desert road, Emerson and Micah stood there facing each other outside of the bus. Finally, Emerson broke the silence, saying, "I hope you know what you're doing. You know they are going to come looking for you. This is going to make you look mighty guilty Micah," Emerson begged.

"I am guilty my dearest friend. I am guilty," he said as they embraced in a hug.

As the bus pulled away, he was hoping against all hope that she would turn to look out the window as they passed. But as he'd already known, she wanted nothing to do with him and so didn't so much as look back. Suddenly he felt like Lot's wife, salt that has forever lost its flavor.

CHAPTER 29

CASEY'S DIARY
ENTRY "LOST"

Dear diary,

Once, when I was five-years old, I sat on the shore of Lake Washington watching the other kids swim and play and enjoy themselves. I hadn't yet passed the lifeguards' swimming test, so I had to stay in the shallow end.

I had tried before, many times. But this time I would succeed. I was determined. All I had to do was swim the distance of about thirty yards, out to the floating logs in the deep end and back, then I would pass the test. I remember waking up that day saying, "today is the day Casey."

So, I waded out to the line and with one last large breath I dove in and began to swim. I swam as if I were born in the water, paddling with all of my might. I didn't even look where I was going. I just kept my head down and swam blindly. And then I felt it. The logs that had evaded me for so long were right there next to me! I had made it! I remember celebrating to myself, thinking 'now I can finally play with the others.' So with that, I began to swim back to the shallow end, but I knew I was in trouble right away. I stopped and looked back at the logs in the distance.

'Could I make it back? No, better to just keep going.'

I remember when I knew for sure I wasn't going to make it. I looked around and didn't see the lifeguard anywhere. I tried to stay afloat, dog paddling for my life. But one wave after another kept sloshing over my head. I wasn't going to make it. I knew I was going to drown. I started choking, coughing up the water as it began to fill my lungs. And then …. I was under. My father was going to be so upset with me. I couldn't breathe … I just couldn't breathe …..

Diary ….. that's how I've felt for weeks now. Unable to breathe. Except this time there's no one to save me. I'm not sure I even want to breathe. The sun has no light, food has no taste, music has no melody.

I sat in the front row of the meeting today so that no one would see my crying. But now, I am all out of tears and words to describe how I feel. I'm numb inside. Most days I don't even get out of bed. The friends encourage me to 'get up, go and do something. This isn't healthy.' But I've spent years taking care of my health and the truth is …. I just don't care anymore.

I don't want to get better. I don't want anything other than to just be left alone.

After the bus ride I was kept in an interview room for what seemed like two days, though it was probably only a few hours. This wasn't how I saw my honeymoon going. I still feel no different than when I had a shackle on my ankle. Still tied down to the bed.

Psychiatrists, psychologists, and pathologists asked me the same questions over and over again, although in different ways each time. I didn't tell them what Micah had told me about planning it all. As much as he hurt me, he had saved me twice and so far as I am concerned, we're even.

But I'll never trust him again.

A nationwide manhunt began for him after he didn't come in for questioning. They'll never find him. He knows how to hide and lie right in plain sight. My father is sending me back to Seattle. I could've fought him but I don't have the energy. Truth is, he's all I have now. We may not always see eye to eye, but at least he's honest. I wish my heart were completely broken so I wouldn't feel this throbbing pain. I was better off when I thought I was crazy. Everything I trusted turned out to be wrong. My life is a fraud. At least when I was crazy I had faith in mankind.

Now, I have no faith, no love to give. I don't even love myself for being so naïve so as to believe him. He wore a ski mask Casey. Get a clue …..

Every goal, every hope, every plan I had for the future circulated around him. Now, what future I have left is sitting in his shadow, dark and lifeless. Truth be told, I don't even know where to place my next step.

CHAPTER 30

TRACKING YAK

Location: Santa Barbara
Time: Day of the bus ride

Cold. It was so cold to Micah as he sat hidden among the orange groves surrounding the warehouse. He wasn't sure why it was so cold all of a sudden. Perhaps it was because it was late fall, or perhaps it was because she wasn't with him. Either way, it was best just to block it out of his mind, as he had serious work to do.

He knew when he'd gotten out of the bus that he would have precious little time to get back to the warehouse before the police arrived. As it was, he was at least 5 miles away. He ran as fast and as far as he could. But ultimately they arrived before he did. Now he sat crouched behind a tree, waiting for them to leave. Hoping that they would leave some evidence behind that would help him to track Yak. The police weren't going to catch him, Micah knew. Yak's motives were different than what they were used to dealing with. The typical things that get most people caught, like sex, drugs, and money, wasn't going to be what brought Yak down. No, he was a different type of animal. And as far as that went, it occurred to Micah while on that bus that he himself was the only one who knew Yak well enough to put all the clues together. That's why Micah hadn't gone down to the police station. It wasn't out of fear of repercussions. It was because every moment he would be held for questioning was another moment Yak was getting away. And considering the police had been looking for him for years now, well, Micah had reason to doubt their abilities. Besides, Casey was his wife now. Whether she hated him or not. Didn't matter. His first concern was her safety and the best way he could do that was to put an end to Yak. One way or the other.

The blue and red strobe lights from the squad cars lit up the night as they processed clues and took photos long into the evening. It was nearly 4 a.m. by the time they left for the night, finally giving Micah a chance to enter for himself.

He went straight for the office that Yak had taken a nap in. Looking around in the darkened room, marked off with crime scene tape and littered with unused 'evidence bags' all over the floor, Micah found what he was looking for right away. A receipt that read, Buddhist Books and Poems ......If you don't buy it now, you may have to wait until your next life." The address pointed to a shop on State Street. That would be a problem as State Street is one of the most busy tourist locations in town. He would need a disguise and this time sunglasses weren't going to be enough.

Location: State Street
Time: Day 2 after warehouse

He knew he must've looked silly wearing that old gray wig and makeup. He probably looked like a cross dresser to them. But he soon calmed down as he entered the store, as he wasn't even close to the strangest person in there.

Walking up to the cashier he asked for books on the reincarnation of mothers. The cashier seemed unconcerned with the request, as though she'd heard many such strange requests.

"You hear that kind of request often do you?" Micah asked.

She looked up from her book and took a moment to size him up. Then, as if all were normal, said, "Yeah.

I hear that one a lot. In fact, I just gave away the last copy of my best book on the subject three days ago."

"Really? Did he or she say why they wanted that specific book? I just thought maybe they were in the same meditation group and thus I could borrow the book from them." "Uh. I doubt this guy does meditation. He's not like you and me. In fact, he said he was going down to the antique store down the street to pick up some things from his past life. Weird guy," she said, while swirling her finger around her ear in the universal sign for 'crazy.' Micah walked into the antique store a few moments later, only to find no one at the register. But, looking around, he found his first clue. Slave trade shackles, $10.00.

He picked up a pair and headed for the counter.

Still no one around. Then he noticed an invoice sitting among some scattered papers. It read. 'Antique shackles delivered to Vino Cottage, Vineyard and Winery.' It was all Micah needed. He took the invoice and went for a long ride on yet another city bus.

He was a fugitive now. Or so he'd heard when he'd called Emerson to see if he could bring his Jeep to him. "I don't think that's a good idea man. The police are crawling all over this place. You'd better stay clear of here," Emerson warned.

Emerson had even mentioned that the local police were going to air his face on America's Most Wanted that very evening.

As Micah looked out of the windows, the passing buildings and streets seemed foreign to him now, even though they had been the source of such great joy just days ago while he was with her. Now though, even the street lamps seemed to glare at him accusingly as they spotlighted him riding in the back of the bus. It was like he was being evicted. As the bus turned away toward the countryside he felt as though the buildings behind were turning their backs on him, as though they too couldn't bear to look at him.

Arriving at the outer fringe of wine country he disembarked, glancing around, wanting to approach the place on foot in case Yak was still there. Yak was so much bigger than Micah. So he had to use speed and stealth if he was to stand a chance.

Upon arriving at the mailbox of the address, he faced his worst fear. There was a chateau at the far end of the vineyard with a clear panoramic view, free of obstruction for 100 yards. "In other words," Micah whispered to himself, "there's no way to approach the house un-noticed." The only cover being the barren rows of vines, thousands of them, leading right up to the entrance. And so it became clear, this was definitely a job for the nighttime.

Location: Vineyard
Time: 2:00 a.m.

Cold. The frozen ground was so cold to him as he belly crawled another 20 feet. The first frost was beginning to form, both on the ground and unfortunately, on him too. Adrenaline rushed through his veins. He was about 45 yards from the building and from what he'd been hearing, there were dogs either inside the house or chained up somewhere near the perimeter. Yet another problem. Each 10 yards he traversed the dogs would go crazy, barking as though they were saying. 'We know you're out there! Don't even try it.' Still, he would have to try it. He had no other choice. Finally, just as the dawn began to break, he made it within 10 yards. The barking was now completely out of control. He knew the owner would be out any minute. But as he approached the house he saw that it was empty. Not just empty, but rather, had been empty for a while. Say 100 years. What he wouldn't have done for those night vision goggles then. He stood up to inspect and …….. "AGRRR ……!!! Let go. Let go!!!" he screamed, swinging blindly at the dog on his leg. He was afraid to look. He'd always had an issue with dogs, ever since he was bitten at the age of four. He swung and flailed at it pointlessly, finally yelling "DOWN!"

That did it. The dog simply let go and sat down. Micah turned to look in horror at his vicious attacker, ready to swing again ...... 'a *poodle?*' Micah stood back, embarrassed. A white .... three pound .....female ..... miniature ..... poodle. She sat there, tail wagging at his feet innocently, as if to say. '*What? Playtime over?*'

"Yes it's over, dangit!" Micah rebuked it, as it cowered at the authority of his voice. "Yeah, well you ought to be ashamed of yourself. You scared me half to death. What do you think you're guarding out here anyway? Fort Knox?" The puppy didn't answer. "Well it's not Fort Knox, it's a vineyard." The puppy's ears perked up. "Vineyard" That got her attention. "Your name is what, Vinny? No. Vin? No. Mini?" The poodle lit up, barking and wagging her tail. "Mini is your name? Ok .... Mini .... if we're going to do this thing you've got to shut up. Mini didn't like that, barking aggressively. "What? Shut up?" Again aggressive barking. "Ok, how about – be quiet. Is that better?" Mini didn't answer, but simply followed along as Micah inspected the house, entering through a vacant wall in the broken structure.

Once inside, he discovered what he had come for. One room, if one could call it that. Really it was just three walls with cold campfire embers at its center, indicating that Yak had indeed been there. But that was the least of the evidence he needed to know. In one corner of the room, lying next to an abandoned sleeping bag, was an envelope. Inside Micah discovered a chilling clue.

Photos. Hundreds of them. All of Casey. He looked them over. The photos weren't taken by Yak. No, they went too far back for that. Who took them? He turned one over, it read, 'My darling daughter, age 4.'

SHEILA!!!!!! Yak wasn't simply following Casey's mom. He knew Sheila personally!

He grabbed the photos in a hurry, looking around to make sure he hadn't missed anything. He needed to get back to Seattle and quick. Emerson's motorbike ought to do, he thought to himself.

As he turned to leave, Mini bit his pant leg. "Gotta go Mini, sorry …." Mini didn't let go. "It's a motorbike, you wouldn't be comfortable." Still Mini held on. "Ok, but don't say I didn't warn ya," he said, as he picked her up and headed for Seattle.

CHAPTER 31

CASEY'S DIARY ENTRY "MOM"

Dear diary,

It took a while to see things clearly, or should I say feel things clearly. But there is one thing that has been my saving grace. Mom. I never knew much about mom. Only that she'd had a problem with addiction to things. Anything she could get a hold of really. Alcohol. Drugs. Abusive men. Things hadn't started out that way for her though. Originally mom and dad were a happily married couple living in Bellevue, Washington.

Mom worked at Microsoft as a programmer while dad finished his studies at the University for his law degree. She became pregnant so they took out a loan to buy their first house. The problem was, the only house they could afford was a house in the Central District, often called the CD. It was a dangerous place, with drive-by shootings and murders weekly.

One day while mom was at the pharmacy getting her prescription of pre-natal vitamins, an armed robber entered the store demanding some type of synthetic heroin. When the cashier re-fused, feeling safe behind the protective glass, the gunman opened fire, wounding my mom and her unborn child.

Mother was rushed to the hospital and saved. But they could not save her baby, who died instantly from a fragment that struck the embryo. That was the first time she ever took a drink. I guess she never did really stop. Eventually she began to try other things, worse things.

Father tried to ignore it (it is his way) figuring that it was just a phase and that she would get over it. But she never came out of it. Things went downhill from there. The marriage was strained to the breaking point, until a miracle happened. Although she was told by the Doctors that she could never give birth again, somehow she was once again pregnant.

For nine long months she was sober, but immediately after I was born, she started up again. The Doctors said it was postpartum depression and that she would recover. But she never did.

The divorce was final by the time I was five. My father went on to bury himself in his work, fighting crime, one case at a time. He was determined to bring about changes to the gun laws. In fact, Micah's case was the first case he'd tried. I guess he was a bit zealous as everyone knew that the sentence was rather harsh considering the circumstances. Mother was nowhere to be found after the divorce. It was as if being around me was too much of a reminder of the other child she'd lost.

Thus, I had not seen nor heard from her until the wedding. But as you know, I had no real time to talk to her before it all went wrong. But today, here back in Seattle, I received an e-mail from her. It read,

'Mom ….. I'd like to talk.'

CHAPTER 32

THE FUGITIVE

The can line alarm rattled to life in the darkened woods of West Seattle's Alki Park, drawing Micah's attention to the perimeter. It was a simple alarm consisting of strung up soda cans containing one pebble each and connected by dental floss weaving between the suspended cans hidden in the tree line forming a 50 yard perimeter.

It was a sad but true fact that this wasn't the first time he'd had to hide from the police which incidentally he had become fairly adept at it over the years.

He laid there in his sleeping bag, being warmed by the heated rocks buried just a few inches below the ground he slept on. The can line had been triggering all night.

'Raccoons' he muttered to himself.

The problem with a can line in that neighborhood was that the shiny metal attracted the curious kits that followed their more focused parents on the night hunts.

But it wasn't the rattling of the coons that had woke him. No. Rather it was the nightmare. The same one he'd had at least once every week for years. The kind that was so scary that he'd force himself awake just to escape. The shot. The same shot that ricocheted off of the wall and killed the man.

He'd try to stop it of course. He always tried to stop it. Diving into the trajectory to stop the bullet. But as usual he would fail, the man would die ..... again ..... and then BOOM! .....he's waiting outside of a room for the judicial committee to tell him to come in.

"Failed again," he whispered to himself. Now those same old options presented themselves in his mind again. Going into the dense depression over what was done, or pretending it's not there, creeping at the corners of his mind. Both options weren't really options at all. They were results. Cause and effect.

Like when he woke up in Alaska after a long night of partying and drinking. But then it quickly became morning and his 'friends' had left him there alone. The streets holding out hope only for continuous cold, cause and effect. He shook his head quickly, trying to stop the familiar course.

He had started the long tour of self-examination, condemnation, years ago. But it never helped. Pen meets paper and suddenly a passing thought becomes a visited regret. As if he needed more of those. Should he have told her the whole story sooner? Would she have married him? Did he trick her into loving him? Their first kiss hung on his lips like a plush dream. He could still taste her tongue, feel the softness of her lips well into the night hours. He laid there staring up at the ceiling made of stars and the tips of fir trees waving in the breeze. He was hooked well before the wedding, but the first kiss had come at the end of the ceremony and had sealed his fate more so than the vows. "And it shall be written on their hearts" he whispered. What was it about a kiss that made things so seemingly real?

He smiled as he recalled their trip to Sea World. He had decided to ask her out formally, she had answered "Why not?"

Why not. One step away from no. Still, he took it.

Addiction does that to people he thought to himself. Gets people to lower their expectations from what they really want, to what they can get. Still, he took it and maybe that was his problem. Maybe he was just more emotionally invested in all of this than she was. Maybe she was just 'settling' for him. He shuddered at the thought.

What was that! The can line clanged to life. Loudly. Micah was up and running through the trees as fast and as quietly as he could go. Flashlights beamed from the southern entrance into the park. It could be campers he thought to himself as he hid behind a copse of trees. Not likely though as it had to be 2 or 3 a.m. Party goers possibly. But from the sound of the keys, even that thought was hopeful thinking.

"Come out! This is the Seattle Police! You are trespassing on government property! Come out! Don't make us go in there!"

Micah smiled. It was the old voice trick that all officers learned in training. They were told that if they demanded the criminal to 'Get down! Hands up! Or Freeze!' then human nature would cause most criminals to obey. They also taught however, that the ones that didn't listen were dangerous and required force, sometimes deadly.

Today, Micah was one of those people. He crept farther away toward the north. Toward the residential area that bordered the park. He had been raised in the West Seattle area and so knew all the ins and outs, the back ways, and alleys rarely traversed. He had just come out of the wooded area and landed into someone's backyard after climbing the fence when he heard, "THERE HE IS!"

That did it. He was up and running again. Weaving between houses as daylight began to break. He wasn't sure if they had actually seen him or had just yelled out to get him to reveal himself. Either way, it had worked.

Most criminals, he knew, would run straight down the middle of a street, foolishly trying to outrun squad cars. It was not only a losing plan, it also swung the odds of capture in the hands of the pursuers. They had cars. Micah preferred a different strategy. Their belts were heavy. If they could jump over ten consecutive fences, outrunning the occasional dog awaiting therein, well then they deserved to catch him. As it was, he had been in many such chases and had never been caught. Today would be no exception he told himself as he hid between two large houses. It didn't sound as if they were getting nearer. They were probably fanning out, creating a perimeter of their own cars, complete with flashing 'red and blue' lights. It didn't matter. He knew where he was going.

He hunched down resting up against a nearby house for support. Unexpectedly, the occupant of one of the houses sheltering him in silence, woke up and came into her living room. Which wouldn't have been a problem if her bay window blinds were shut. They weren't.

He sat there, dressed in black. In plain view of her while she sipped on a steaming cup of something. It was a good thing he had dropped off Mini at an old friend's house, as by now Mini would be throwing a fit as the lady bent over to pick up her cat. Then something got her attention. She went to the front door and looked out. Micah could just barely make out the stripes of a squad car as it passed down the street, slowing as she waved from her front porch. Satisfied, she watched as the car moved on. Unfortunately, her continued curiosity brought her to look out her side window. There, their eyes met. Face to face. Only her window separating the two. He brought his index finger up to his lips. '*Shhhh*' he motioned.

She did the opposite. Hurriedly slamming the front door shut and dead bolting it.

"Great," Micah quipped, no longer whispering as he took off running again, having heard the squad car put it in reverse. It didn't matter really. They wouldn't catch him. Couldn't catch him. He needed to find Yak. And to find Yak, he'd have to remain free. To remain free he'd have to run.

So, he ran.

By mid-afternoon the adrenalin had long since worn off. The chase sputtered off after a spirited beginning.

After all, they were simply chasing a trespasser in their minds. Not someone wanted for questioning in a kidnapping. Had they known that about their rabbit they may even have called out the 'yard bird' as some in the ghetto called a helicopter.

The thought tickled him as he approached Pier 51 in downtown Seattle wearing sunglasses (without the UV sticker this time). This was a familiar trip. One he had traveled a hundred times as a youngster. He would creep out of his bedroom just after his mother went to sleep, walk down the street and another three miles to the bus stop.

Catching a bus heading downtown, he would get off near the Pike Place Market. The Market had many levels to it. The most famous being the Fish Market where everything from huge Monk fish to Red Cod could be sold. During the day time Jazz musicians would play live on the corners while tourists would gape and stare at the skill of the fish throwers tossing 10 pound fresh salmon through the air like pizza dough in the window.

But that wasn't why Micah was there that day. No, he had far more important things on his mind. Still, the sound of Jimmy Hendrix being played expertly by a nearby saxophonist gave him pause as he descended the steps down several floors, finally emerging at Seattle's bustling waterfront.

It looked different in the daytime and his mission would be far more dangerous than his usual child-hood rendezvous. His target was not just to make it to Pier 51. Rather it was a special spot on that pier. His spot. Well, his and Jehovah's.

He only came here when he was desperate. When he needed an answer. This is where he came to pray. Problem was, his spot to pray was not *on* Pier 51. It was *under* it.

Seattle was actually built upon the ashes of an older version of Seattle that had burned down years ago.

Many of the current buildings were built on top of older buildings buried beneath them.

Under Pier 51 was water, of course. But if one cared to investigate, one would find a ladder descending down into that water and on the second to last rung there was a beam. A beam that connected to and older, long since forgotten pier.

Pier 51 minus 1, Micah called it. It was his spot. Where he went to shut out the world. Where else could someone be absolutely alone in a metropolis?

He walked up to the edge of the pier and looked around.

A fisherman in the corner. Lovers whispering closely sitting on a bench. A city worker sweeping up trash in his dustpan while listening to music on his headphones.

Micah slipped over the edge expertly. No one noticed. Had anyone seen him go over, they would've screamed, probably thinking suicide was on his mind. But, as it was, all was clear.

"Well, Jehovah. I'm here. I know I've done a lot of things wrong. Believe me, I know. But that's no reason for her to have to suffer. Father, I need to find him and stop him. I'm not sure if I'm going about this the right way and I know I will have to pay for my mistakes, but for right now I just need for her to be safe. Once I am absolutely sure she is safe and will remain safe, I will turn myself in for questioning. I will obey the superior authorities after I obey your laws. And your laws are clear. I am to treat my wife as Christ treated the congregation. Christ protected his disciples on the night of his arrest. I must protect her. She is staying with her father and she is wearing the old shoes I put tracking devices in, so I know where she is. But Yak is out there planning. So far he has been efficient at catching me off guard. I know about your law about a 'goring bull.'

The law said that if a person has a bull that is known to gore people and he lets it loose after knowing its nature then that man is responsible if the bull kills someone. Well, Jehovah, I let lose this bull, Yak, and he has to be put back in his pen! I am asking for your help, Jehovah, please!

Remember Samson? How he knew he was at fault for his situation? Yet he prayed to you for power. Power that he knew would end in his death. I ask you now for that same power, intelligence, and endurance. Whatever is necessary to put the bull back in the pen. Please. You are my only hope. In the name of your Son, Jesus Christ, Amen."

CHAPTER 33

CASEY'S DIARY
"Mom Is Cool"

Dear diary,

She was everything I have ever wanted in a mother, at least for the first hour of our visit. Then she took her first drink. I had been expecting it at least. Dad had kept me up until midnight the night before, warning me about what to expect. He meant well and to his credit, he didn't go so far as to try to convince me not to go, well, openly anyway. I could tell he was worried.

Maybe he was worried that I would love her more or that she would paint him as the bad guy in the divorce. And that, ultimately, I would end up loving her more than him and perhaps never come back. But that wasn't going to happen. Frankly, I understood all the sacrifices he'd made for me. He'd even kept my room untouched from when I'd left to move down to California. I guess he was hoping I would come back someday.

It was a bit weird to step back into my old room the way it was. It was like stepping out of a time machine, having traveled back to the year 2000. But admittedly, it was comforting to climb back into my old bed, under my own blankets. Even my old shoes fit. And it had been years since I played that old guitar. I gave it a try for a few moments but had to put it down. I have emotionally recovered somewhat. But not that far.

Christina is married now to some logger. They moved to Snoqualmie to start a family. In fact, most of my old friends and classmates have all moved on. While I somehow moved back both physically and metaphorically.

I don't even say his name. Will not. If I were to speak to him again, I'm afraid that what would come out of my mouth would be anything other than Christian. He had played the hero when really he was the perpetrator. He began all of this and what's worse ..... he made me love him for it. CRAZY.

Whatever happened to the good old boring men? People who were boring but truthful. I mean, look at my mom. She is a hopeless alcoholic. An HONEST hopeless alcoholic. That I can accept. Yak? Yak was crazy, sure. But he was also right. I had been played just like that guitar in the corner. Difference is, when I'm finished playing it I put it down and it's undamaged.

Oh ….. got another e-mail from mom. Let's see …… it says she wants to spend the day together Friday. Cool. She says it'll be a tea party. I just hope it's not the 'Long-Island' variety.

CHAPTER 34

CASEY'S DIARY ENTRY: FRIDAY

Dear diary,

Where do I begin? Friday morning started out just as any other I guess. Save for the anticipation of seeing my mother again. The rain was coming down sideways as it usually does in the winter. The weather report said we could expect some rain partially mixed with snow over the weekend. I'm not putting chains on just yet, as the Seattle rain always seems to wash away the snow just before it can stick.

Got to mom's apartment around 10:00 a.m. That's about where normal stopped.

First thing out of the norm was the sticky note stuck to the front door that read .... 'Casey, come on in, the door is unlocked.'

Guess I should've been more cautious but the apartment is in the middle of downtown Seattle, so I figured if anything strange were going on inside, one of the neighbors would've reported it. And by now there'd be police everywhere, right? Well, if you believe that one then we would both be wrong, as I was that morning.

I entered into the apartment and looked around. Everything seemed to be in its natural place. Same as the last visit. The TV was on, the apartment was clean and orderly. There was even the fresh smell of the tea that I love so much. Chamomile, my favorite. Really, the only thing that was missing was mom. I picked up the phone: "Dad? Did mom call to tell you she was going to be late?"

"No Case, why, she isn't there?" he asked, not seeming surprised at all.

"No dad, just a note that said 'come in."

"Well Case, she probably just ran to the store, just hang tight."

So that's what I did. I just sort of wandered around the apartment until I found myself sitting on her bed in her room. And that's when I saw them.

Pictures. There must have been hundreds of them. Pictures of me stuck to her vanity mirror, in stacks on her night stand, and even one huge blown up picture of me at my high school graduation in poster form.

As I perused over them I found pictures I didn't even know were taken, pictures from school plays, with dad on the campaign trail and even one of me sitting in a high chair, eating of all things, carrots.

I had no idea. Dad had apparently taken some of them. But the majority she must've taken herself. He had always told me that he didn't know where she was, but I found a receipt in an old shoebox along with some legal papers that indicated dad was actually named on the lease. He had been paying for the apartment the entire time! I guess he never forgot those years that she worked to provide for them while he was in law school.

In another box I found stacks of envelopes. There must have been more than 200. All of them addressed to me:

Dear Casey, you're turning ten today. Wish I could be there. But when I see the newest pictures of you, I can see that you are so happy. With that smile that just lights up your whole face. I know you are safe. I just wanted to send you this letter to let you know that I'm thinking of you. To let you know that I've always loved you and always will. And though I am not there with you in person, I am with you in spirit. Love, mom

                Hugs and carrots. Xoxo

The letters were not postmarked. She never sent them. I went through three or four letters that sounded just like that. Most written on my birthday or Christmas. A bunch of others were written in slightly different handwriting, maybe she was on something at the time. But those were the ones I liked the most. They were raw, but I understood what she'd meant. How she felt. I've been feeling the same way as of late. I felt a mix of emotions reading them there on her bed. Angry that I was never told how nearby she was. Sad that she never got up the courage to mail them. But most of all love. Love for a mother that I never had, but somehow, always had. I didn't make it through many more before the tears started to flow and the floodgates of all those years wondering, were opened up and filled with those few sheets of paper. I guess with all that emotion going on I didn't notice the envelope sitting on her pillow that simply read: 'CASEY'

Dear Casey,

First I want you to know that I love you more than life itself and that I have always loved you, my daughter. How quickly the years have passed and my sincerest intentions of visiting you passed with them.

It seems the only time I ever got up the courage to come and see you was when I was on a bender at 2:00

a.m. I would come knocking on your door and your dad would tell me 'Not now, Sheila, not like this. She thinks you are an angel. Do you want her to see you like this and destroy her innocent heart? Wait till morning, fix yourself up a bit then come to see her.' It made me feel so low that each time I had to be more drunk than the time before just to stand on your porch.

I guess he was right, he always knew best. I want you to know that your father loves you and that he is not at fault for any of this. He ….. we, decided that it was best to wait till I was sober to visit you. But I'm so weak my daughter, not like you. I'm so weak and pitiful that it took years just to get to a place where I could look at myself in the mirror again. To face what I had done.

I'm just so ashamed. What your father never knew all those years, what I never told him, was that I couldn't love him because I couldn't love myself. He never knew that I was responsible for the death of your brother.

When that robber entered the store and asked for the drugs, it was I who grabbed for his gun. I don't even know why I did it. I was courageous, feisty and bold in those days. Yeah, you get it from me. Never lose that my daughter. Never let anyone turn you into a victimized turtle, hiding under a shell as I am today. Back then I thought I could conquer the world and I guess I was so incensed that this man would have the audacity to rob a place where the sick and helpless go to get help. Preying on the weak like that. I just couldn't standby and take it.

We had already named him. Your brother. Tracy. After he died I just couldn't look in the mirror anymore. I didn't know what to do. And then I got pregnant with you. You were feisty even before you were born. Kicking every time we played 'Young at Heart,' it was a song that was popular in my time, you've probably never heard of it. You kicked whenever your father spoke and you seemed to fall asleep to Beethoven.

But after you were born I again went into my shell. I guess I feared that when you got older and heard that I had been pregnant before, you'd never forgive me if I told you the truth. I wanted you to be my friend as well as my daughter. But instead, I turned to the only friend I had. The bottle. I have made so many poor decisions in my lifetime. But maybe the worst one of them all was the decision I made yesterday.

You have to understand that he listened to me and was so kind to me. I didn't realize he was the one you guys were running from. Yak. He's here now. Sitting at the table while I write this letter to you. He made me tell him everything, including about your grandfather's cabin near Mt. St. Helen's.

Do you remember the place? We used to go there camping on the weekends, those days that I was out of re-hab.

It's an old log cabin sitting all alone at the bottom of a ridge near a river. That's where he's taking me. He says if you come, he will let me go. He says that if you call the police he will kill me. He says he has police scanners and he will be listening to all radio traffic for any hint of trouble. He's telling me that you are to tell your father that you are going camping for the weekend with me. That we just need a little time together. He also says he won't hurt either of us and that it is a fair exchange. Mother for mother. Whatever that means. When I told him to write this letter himself, he said that it would be better coming from me. But I think the real reason is that he can't read or write. So, risking that, I will now conclude this letter with my own words:

Casey, don't come. If I was ever going to be your mother, if you would ever have obeyed me, then listen to your mother now! Don't come! I have had the greatest moment of my life already ..... seeing you born, just knowing you are safe is enough for me to die in peace. And, if your religion is true, then maybe I will see you again someday. I love you, my darling daughter.

Love, mom

Hugs and carrots, xoxo

Tears flowed once again. But now it was turning to anger. A deep seated anger that I had never felt before. Enough is enough. This monster has gone too far. He has attempted to destroy everything I have ever cared for or believed in. Mom was mistaken about one thing. I would never have blamed her for the death of the baby. Sometimes people make mistakes. Sometimes those mistakes are irreversible, but, all the same, love covers a multitude of sins. Not only do I not blame her, I probably would've done the same thing, minus the drinking afterwards. She knew back then what I am only just now beginning to figure out. And that is you just cannot sit around and let other people mold your life. Victimizing you for their will and purpose. She was right! The audacity of such a man! The audacity of Yak! He not only kidnapped my mom, but he has the audacity to presume that I will meekly obey his rules like a good little victim.

"OH I'M COMING YAK!! AND IN THE WORDS OF WYATT EARP, 'HELL WILL COME WITH ME!!!'"

There is this passage in the Bible where Abraham is going to sacrifice his son Isaac. So he gets to this mountain and he tells his servants that he and his son are going up that mountain and that they will return. Now what intrigued me about this passage is that Abraham knows he is going to sacrifice his son, yet so great is his faith that God will resurrect his son, that he tells the attendants, in effect, 'we'll be right back.'

This is the type of faith necessary to succeed when life and death hang in the balance, as it does now. So in my letter to dad, I simply said,

Dad, I love you but I'm going to visit with mom for a while.

We will be right back.

Hugs and carrots, xoxo
Love, Casey

I do not know how long it will be before dad begins to panic, but if he knows my mom as well as I think he does, well, I guess we'll have to wait and see.

Nevertheless, I am an adult, and with this letter in hand, he will not be able to involve the police without proof of foul play. Besides, this is a job for me as much as it is for my mother. Still, no reason a girl should go out un-prepared.

The one thing my father and I had in common was our love for the outdoors. Every summer we would go camping. At first he tried to take me hunting, but after I threw a fit over a buck he killed, throwing myself on it while begging God to bring it back to life, well .... needless to say he was content to stick with fishing from then on.

We have crazy mad camping gear: K-2 all-weather sleeping bags, climbing gear, waterproof matches and flashlights. Oh, and M.R.E.'s, which is to say, Meals Ready To Eat, complete with a magnesium packet surrounded by hardened calcium nitrate that when broken and added to water, causes a chemical reaction that heats up the food package. All this according to dad, who excitedly told and re-told the story every time we ate one. But maybe the most important tool I will be taking is his 30/06 Remington Long Range Rifle with scope. All of which made me look a bit like Rambo if he were trying to scale Mt. St. Helen's in pink.

Mt. St. Helen's is of course mostly known for its outburst back in 1980. What few people know is that the lava and ash that came down with it later enriched the soil to such a degree that now the foothills of the mountain boast some of the most spectacular wildflowers and animal life, but now there's a new type of animal in those hills, Yak. So the rifle is a necessary evil.

The plan is simple. The ridge is where I'll set up camp. From there I can watch the cabin and wait. The cabin is something you usually only see in books. Picturesque, but old, with no indoor plumbing. I'd begged grandpa to update the place but he'd say, "This place has been round since fore you was born and be round long afta me and you, sides, it adds character, doncha think?" No, I didn't think. There was nothing like the experience of running out into the snow at 3:00 a.m. to the outhouse, only to find you had forgotten to bring paper.

Well, that was back then and this is now. And now it was going to play to my advantage. Sooner or later Yak would have to ease nature and when he takes that thirty yard trip ..... pow! Goodbye Yak. Then, if all goes well ..... I scale down the cliff, enter the cabin, find the SAT phone (a satellite phone) which dad gave grandpa to use in case of an emergency which grandpa once did indeed use when he ran out of beer in December. When dad said it wasn't a true emergency, grandpa had said, "wait till you're my age, a winter socked in without beer out here is a true emergency." When dad said that only life and death was an emergency, grandpa countered with "that's not an emergency, that's nature." (As things would have it, grandpa did indeed die in that cabin the following year, incidentally, with a beer in his hand.)

Anyway, I'll use the SAT phone to call dad, grab mom and scale back up the cliff using pulleys and harnesses that I've brought, then hike the two miles back to my car. Signed, sealed and delivered.

CHAPTER 35

WINTER WONDERLAND

The snow had just begun to fall as she turned off I-5 South onto Toutle Road. Toutle River has its water source high on the mountain she knew, as she had been swimming in it one summer and got the shock of her life with just how cold it had been.

The river winds its way on the eastern side of St. Helen's, carving a path around snow crested hills and canyons until finally it finds its way past her grandfather's cabin.

During the summer she had enjoyed the good fishing, brook trout mostly, but during the winter it could freeze in places so thick that the hunters often crossed while still riding their four-wheelers.

One had to be careful crossing it, as it was known to be the death of many an unwary hunter, who had irreversibly overestimated the ice shelf.

What mattered most, Casey knew, was the current under the water. So the places one would think were the safest to cross, say for instance an expanse of just 5 feet, in reality, because the current speeding up in those areas, the ice is in fact much thinner than a wider expanse would've been.

She mapped all of this out in her mind as she got out of the car. She was already regretting having not put on chains, as the snow was starting to pile up. A fact she noticed just 20 yards down the trail when she looked back and already found she could no longer see her recent prints. "Well, too late now ...." she whispered as she began the ascent to the cliff overhang.

Somehow though, the snow always made her feel at peace, both with herself and with nature, it had a way of dampening all sounds to a soft whisper. It reminded her of the stories she would write as a child about being with her special snow-angel-mother in a winter wonderland. Well, she would be with her mother but it would be a different type of wonderland to be sure.

The hike to the ridge was turning out to be far more daunting than she had anticipated. A recent mudslide had wiped out the old path, so she found herself going a round-about way that nearly got her lost, the usual landmarks having been hidden in the fresh snow. Finally reaching the ridge just before dusk, she had her first view of the situation through the scope. "All seems normal," she whispered. The cabin had fresh smoke billowing from its stack and it appeared that a path had been partially cleared from the porch on the far side. It was impossible to know for sure as the cliff was on the backside of the cabin. To all indications, it appeared that mother and Yak were indeed inside. Tomorrow, she thought to herself, I will go down there and get a closer look. Tonight it was too risky to try an attempt. Albeit a descent, still, it would be nearly impossible to see the foot holds on the way down in this light.

She knew she had at least a little time. It wouldn't make sense for Yak to kill her mother having become impatient. At least not after he went through all of that work. That would end the game prematurely and without his prize. "Oh, you'll get your *prize* Yak," she muttered as she erected the tent just a few yards back from the cliff edge and safely out of view from the cabin below.

She waited there in the tent as the night temperatures began to drop outside. It seemed funny to her that she had always been told that rock climbing was a dangerous sport and quite pointless. It seemed to make perfect sense that now her skills at it may just end up saving someone's life. Besides, she was by far the most careful rock climber of them all. Always using double ropes and harnesses. The worst that could ever happen, she figured, was that a piton could break loose and she could then drop 5 feet or so before the extra safety rope would catch her, causing quite a rope burn but nothing more serious than that.

She laid there most of the night wondering if she wasn't being at least a tiny little bit hypocritical with him. After all, she had quickly forgiven her mother and that apology had not even come face to face.

He had concealed vital information true, but the engagement and marriage had happened so quickly there was no way to know if they'd had more time to get to know each other maybe he would have said it sooner or later. She pondered that thought while going over her check list, which always seemed to calm her nerves.

"Hmmm. 2 ax hammers, 2 slip stops, 2 pitons, 1 pneumatic nail gun, 2 Sterno fuel propellant burners ……. Oh! MRE's." She ripped open a bag and watched with fascination as the chemical reaction emitted steam into the tent, warming it up a bit. She tried to eat it. It wasn't bad stuff, boiled mixed vegetables, but somehow her stomach just wouldn't work with her. As cool as she was trying to be, the fact was she was scared and nervous. Truth be told, when it came right down to it, she wasn't even sure she could pull the trigger at the critical moment. Still ….. she couldn't bring herself to say his name.

It was as if saying it would open up a box of emotions that would require action. Actions she wasn't quite ready to take. She reached in her bag and pulled out her emergency emotional help.

Dear Casey,

You turned twelve today. Wish I could've been there with you. I've been in Vegas for the last two years working as a waitress. The men are scum, but the tips aren't bad. I think of you every day and every night. But it's the nights that are hard, having you so far away. I want you to know that you are the very best part of me in every way. You are the best thing I ever achieved, the best goal I ever strived for, the best hope I ever dared to dream. One day we will meet again. I hope you can forgive me for the past and we can just sit and watch the sun go down over the Nevada desert together, as I do every night thinking of you.

Father always said, 'you can choose your job, you can choose your mate, but you can't choose your parents.' Guess that is a hard fact that both you and I have to face. I wish things could've worked out differently sometimes, but then I think of you and how you were conceived in what was most definitely my darkest hour. I wonder, if I hadn't been in such a bad place, would God have really given me an angel like you to save me? But the game of 'what if' is a web of lies in all directions my darling. We can never go back. I guess the point is ..... you're twelve now ..... face it and move on.

Love, mom

Hugs and carrots, xoxo

Morning came quickly as she rolled out of her sleeping bag and unzipped the flap. "Great" she complained a little too loudly. The snow had piled up overnight. One look and she knew that her car had to be buried. She had to go to Plan B, which she'd have to think up at some point.

She began unraveling the ropes. First the descent rope and then the secondary safety rope. The pneumatic air gun snapped to life, loudly firing a piton spike deep into the ledge. Quickly, Casey peered through the scope. No movement. Maybe the snow was a blessing, dampening the sound. She began her descent, hand over hand, lowering herself a few feet at a time while firing pitons into the rock face and clamping off at intervals. Already, her emergency pack waited for her below, as she had thrown it first over the ledge. It was best to prepare for anything. A lesson *someone* had taught her once. The problem was, she was afraid to throw the gun over the edge, as it would probably break on impact. She'd considered lowering it by rope, but every moment spent delayed openly exposed on the rock face, was yet another opportunity Yak had to look out of the window and catch her mid-plan. So she opted for speed and with a silent prayer, left the gun behind.

One problem she hadn't considered when coming up with this reconnaissance run, was that the snow was deep enough to leave prints. Prints that would easily be discovered by Yak if he came out and walked around the cabin, those prints would lead back to the base of the cliff, and in turn, her. But the snow was still falling, so she hoped that it would cover her tracks before any damage could be done. Besides, the mission was for not if she couldn't verify her mother was actually in the cabin. For all she knew, Yak could've paid for a hotel room for her, and mom was actually miles away having a drink in a lobby somewhere. At least that's what she told herself, as she struck out towards the cabin in the early morning sunlight.

Why hadn't she at least called Emerson to say where she was. As careful as she had been lately, she was beginning to notice definite gaps in her logic the closer she got to the cabin. And what if he didn't really have police scanners at all? No, you're right mom.

Now is not the time for the what if game. Coming over a knoll, she came jogging down the valley to her old familiar fishing hole. It looked frozen alright, but she could hear the ice rumble and crack underneath. Sounds she never heard when the ice was good and thick. The river is at least 5 feet deep at its center, she calculated. But it was at least twenty feet across at the juncture she'd begun to walk on. 'Have faith Case …..' she mumbled as she took her first few precarious steps. So far so good. The ice began complaining noisily at the halfway point, and she thought of running for it. But running actually places more weight on one foot than the other. It was best to just 'take it slow Case…….' She chided herself.

Thankfully there was an old tree that had helped her for the first 20 feet. It was an old, dead Aspen that was leaning over the river far enough so that it served as sort of a handrail for her. But now, out in the middle, she was reminded of the swim back from the log at age 5. 'Faith, Case, faith. We'll be right back.' Ten feet from safety, she suddenly realized that she was wearing her 50 lb. emergency pack on her back. Stupid, she thought, should've thrown it across to begin with, yet now, she knew it was too late to try it. The ice was holding her for now, but by the sounds of its protests, the added pressure of her launching the bag may just be enough for her to break through.

After what was probably an hour, just to walk those few yards, she safely reached the bank. Beginning the hike toward the cabin, she turned periodically to look behind her. No one. She knew who she was looking for, and was secretly hoping to find, but each time she turned ..... nothing. She was truly alone.

The cabin sat in a meadow just 30 yards in a clearing from the forest tree line, thus, the last place to hide before the point of no return, was where she was crouching at that moment. There it was. Fresh smoke billowing from the stack, indicating that at the very least, someone had woken up and stoked the fire. She knelt down behind a snow covered bush at the edge of the tree line. 'Well, are we going to do this or what? Come on Casey ...... just think of your worst fear, and that's what's going to happen if you don't take the next step.' It was a trick she'd learned to say to herself when she was in a tough spot while rock climbing. It usually worked because her worst fear had changed.

'Micah'

She almost couldn't believe it had come out of her mouth. But it was true and she knew it. Pushing it to the back of her mind, she broke from the clearing, red hair flailing like a girl on fire, sprinting in the snow with high steps and leaps. Finally, she arrived at the cabin, ducking for cover against the far wall just under the back pantry window. She sat there crouching in the snow, afraid to look inside. What if Yak was in the pantry at the time and just so happened to look out right as she was looking in? Game over Case. But she needed to stop second guessing herself. Really, the only decision she was regretting was the huge pink jacket she was wearing. "Smart Case, you're a real camouflage expert." She whispered. But what if mom is being tortured or worse right at this moment? Thinking back she remembered her rock climbing teacher and what he'd said when she was stuck halfway up a cliff. He'd said, "I don't know what you want to do kid. Go up or go down. But one thing is for sure, you can't stay here. That did it. Casey popped her head up and took a look inside. No. It's not possible. She sat there, crouched, wondering if she had really seen what she'd seen. Another look couldn't hurt. Yup. It was for real ..... just like a scene out of a Dr. Suess book. Mom sat with her back to the window, shackled around one ankle, beer in one hand, photo album in the other, telling stories. They sat there cross legged on the throw rug in front of the fire. It was just as she'd read about in those stories of 'chestnuts roasting on the open fire,' comfortable and cozy on a cold winter's day.

Well, good to see grandpa's good beer isn't going to waste, she thought to herself. She sat there at the window watching the scene like Scrooge looking in on a different life course. The scene was so strange, so ...... surreal...... that she didn't notice the growling until it was too late. She had grown up in these woods on those summers when her dad was too pre-occupied with his campaign to watch her. So she knew better than to be carrying around a backpack full of food in the middle of winter, still, the whole 'mom' ordeal had thrown off her usual outdoorsy instincts. Deservedly, she thought to herself, a pack of wolves shows up right when I'm at my most vulnerable.

No, she couldn't see them yet, but that wasn't unusual, as wolves hunt in packs. By the time you hear the first growl, you're usually already surrounded. You just don't know it yet. That is, until you try to run. Then they come out of the forest from all directions. Their favorite move is the ambush. One wolf would chase you around, not trying to actually catch you. No, he's just trying to tire you out. Then he'll hand you off to the next wolf, usually his best friend, who will also try to wear you out. Then, the lead wolf comes in. He's the actual one who bites you, but not until after he's led you directly into an ambush full of his hungriest friends. Casey had seen this actually happen at an early age. It was when her friend was attacked. The girl had been walking around with a slice of pizza in the dead of winter, just outside of their winter cabin. The wolves were on her before she knew it.

The way Casey saw it, she had just two options. The wolves hadn't yet attacked because she was next to the cabin, they knew cabin = hunters = guns. But if she moved away from the cabin, well ….. she'd have moments before the pack would break from their hiding places in the tree line. So, the question was, could she make it across the river and to the rope dangling at the base of the cliff?

The other option was worse. Knock on the door and go in. What else?

Hmmm ….. her first two strides started so quickly she even caught herself by surprise. She wasn't even sure at what point she'd made up her mind on it. One moment she's next to the cabin, the next, she's fifty feet away and distancing. No doubt the wolves were shocked also, as she was at least ninety yards from the cabin before she heard the first one closing in behind her.

Nearly floating over the snow toward the river, she ran faster than she ever imagined possible. But as she neared the river, she heard the familiar muted sound of paws leaping through the snow and closing. And there she was again, right back in the water at the age of five. Too far from the shore again …. My dad is going to be so upset, I'm not going to make it ……..

CHAPTER 36

LAVA TUBE

It was noon before he picked up her trail. Fresh boot prints deep in the snow leading away from the cabin. Had he known he was going to the North Pole he would've dressed in something other than tennis shoes and a wind breaker. But as it was, he had just been following the red blinking dot blindly down the interstate for the last eight hours. Yet another time he was proud of the fact he had put more than one tracking device in her shoes, so many years ago. Then too, there was the fact that she still wore the same size as when she was seventeen. That had helped a lot in finding her, as the other phone, the one he'd used to track her with the knife, was long since gone and probably sat in some evidence box at the police department in Santa Barbara.

He'd tried several roads before he finally struck upon the one that led to the cabin, so there was no telling where she was until just at that moment when he saw her prints in the snow. Problem was, he still hadn't seen her car. So maybe she drove and found some other way in, or ….. she didn't drive at all because she was in trouble ….. again. He had come in from the eastern side of the mountain and parked next to an old Volvo which had been there long enough to be completely snowed in at the end of the trail. He was just moments from knocking on the cabin door when he looked down and saw that her red dot was moving away at speed.

At least he wasn't alone, that is until just a moment ago, when Mini took off running, just after they'd reached the cabin. She was far too fast for Micah to keep up with. So he trailed behind at a leisurely pace, seeing as Mini's paw prints were now falling directly into Casey's deeper boot prints. He chuckled, as the little puppy disappeared from sight into one of the prints, then came bouncing back out again like a miniature deer.

He had just been finishing off some fries that he'd gotten from McDonald's up the highway, when Mini took off running. There did seem to be an urgency in the pup, Micah thought, so he picked up the pace a little himself. Their tracks rose up over a small hill and down the other side, just past the cabin and tree line. He followed until he found a straight flat path covered in snow and ice. "Hmmmmm. What did you find girl?" he asked Mini, who was wagging her tail at a strange opening in the snow. "What is it girl, whatcha got?" Mini barked, as Micah took a few steps forward.

Ice. He should've recognized it right away. That was why the snow seemed so smooth on the strip. Mini was out on top of a frozen river.

"Come here girl ..." Micah called. He didn't even want to attempt to cross the frozen river, not knowing how deep it was or how thick. But Mini didn't move. Rather, she became all the more insistent, barking louder and louder.

"Ok Mini, this better be worth it," he counseled, as he cautiously stepped onto the ice. A few secure steps and Mini began to go nuts, as if something was really wrong. "What's the matter Mini? Someone tell you to shut up?" And then he saw it .... halfway across the ice, at a spot where it was broken through, was a branch from an Aspen tree. Its tip was bobbing in the water as though there were a fish on the other end. Strange? PINK!!! "CASEY!!!" A small pink hand was holding onto the end of the branch. Casey was under!

He took two long strides before diving belly first onto the ice, sliding to a stop at the opening.

"I got you babe!" he said, desperately yanking on her coat sleeve. "Let go of the branch, babe!!! Let go Casey!!!" She had a death grip on the thing. Frustrated, he gave up on that strategy and instead smashed a fist into the ice, breaking the opening wider. There she was. Just under the surface, barely holding on. He reached down and in a bear hug type move, wrenched her soaking wet body from the icy grave. She fell limp into his arms, unmoving.

"Come on Casey! No! Not like this baby!"

She was now on top of him with her back to him in his lap. Her violent red hair swept over his face as she remained lifeless. Micah snatched her limp body up as though she were a bag of sugar, throwing her over his shoulder, running as he went down the riverside looking for a spot to cross back over to the cabin.

Finding nothing but thinner and thinner ice, he spotted Casey's earlier footprints leading off somewhere else away from the cabin. Instinctively, he followed them.

Coming to the base of the cliff, he found the ropes. "Impossible," he complained. "Casey, I can't get up there. Wake up babe, tell me where to go," he pleaded, while she remained unresponsive.

"What is it Mini?" Micah asked, as Mini started barking and heading off around the side of the cliff. Following Mini, he dis-covered a small lava cave at the base of the cliff. It was dark and foreboding but he had no choice. He knelt down and dragged Casey inside.

"Ok Casey, I've got to take this off of you," he said hopelessly as he took off her backpack.

Thankfully, the backpack had been waterproof, as she had gone under wearing it, and it was probably the reason she couldn't get out. The current below the ice pushed her under, and the backpack served as a hook, keeping her down, clinging to the underside of the ice whenever she tried to lift herself up out of it. He knew what he had to do, stripping her of every stitch of clothing in seconds and shoving her into the sleeping bag, he then set to work on the MRE's. "Now Casey we're gonna get you warm ok? You don't have to do anything, just come back to me babe," he pleaded, hoping she could hear him.

He began breaking open one, then two, then three MRE packets, mixing up the reaction and after sealing the bags, threw them in with her. Stripping himself naked also, having noticed her pink coat had soaked his clothes through with all the contact, he climbed in with her, wrapping her up in a bear hug.

It was the longest twenty minutes of Micah's life, but finally she started coughing and shaking.

"Hang in there babe. I got ya," he said, wrapping her tighter as she mumbled in response.

"Did you say something, babe?" he asked.

"Ya .... You're .... la....la...late," she stuttered.

"Nice to see you too," he teased, squeezing her tighter.

"Wa .... What are you do ... doing here?" She was starting to warm up, giving him hope again.

"Keeping a promise."

CHAPTER 37

TRAPPED

"Sme …. Smells …." She stuttered, moving in closer to his embrace.

"What babe? What smell?"

"MRE's …. The sme …smell .. of the food," she continued.

He was worried. Each breath she took in speaking was abnormally large. He could feel her chest expanding as she struggled to talk. He knew it was a sign of the later stages of severe hypothermia, the lungs were beginning to close in on themselves, making it hard to speak. Soon, her blood would leave all of her extremities in a last ditch effort to conserve heat. At that point, brain damage could ensue.

"You're safe now babe. Conserve your energy," he pleaded.

"Wolves."

"What?"

"The wolves can smell it. MRE's," she said, becoming more persistent.

"There aren't any wolves babe. Wait …. What are you talking about?"

"I was being chased by wolves. That …. That's why I ran ….
fell …. ice."

"Uh, babe. I followed your prints clear to the spot you fell in. there weren't any wolf prints. Just yours and …. oh … Mini."

"Who?"

"Mini," he said, feeling a bit responsible.

"Mini?" she asked, as Mini came over, licking her face upon hearing her name.

"You?" Casey asked, looking strangely at the pup as though it were an alien. "You scared me to death!" she bellowed, suddenly gaining her voice, as Mini whimpered at the rebuke.

"Yeah …. uh …. she has a habit of doing that, I'm trying to break her out of it," he admitted.

"So Casey. What brings you to this neck of the woods?" he asked, trying to perk her up.

"Yak." She countered plainly.

"Where is he?" he asked, growing nervous and wondering how nearby he was.

"In the cabin. Kidnapped mom to lure me here. You didn't know?" she asked, surprised. "No babe. I was tracking you."

"How? I thought the knife phone was back in California?"

"Elasmobranchology," he answered, as though it should be obvious.

"Elasmo ….. What?"

"Elasmobranchology is the study of sharks. Back when I was thirteen, my dad took the whole family back to Guam."

"Where?"

"Guam, that's where your husband is from babe. Anyway he promised to teach me to surf. So there we were in the ocean, floating on our boards when suddenly we hear someone screaming. We didn't see where it was coming from and as I looked around for a while I noticed I didn't know where dad was either. Then I saw him, about fifty yards away, dragging something from the surf. It turned out to be a boy about my age, missing an arm. After he was taken to the hospital some reporters interviewed my dad and I'll never forget what he said."

"What?" she asked, forgetting the cold.

"He said, 'Wasn't the sharks fault. We were just in the wrong place at the wrong time."

"I sat and wondered about that comment all that night. If we were in the wrong place I wondered, where was the right place? So I decided I would learn more about sharks. Thing is, it's hard to really study sharks out of the water. Sure we can learn about their anatomy and other things, but to truly understand them we have to know what they are doing in their natural habitat. So marine biologists invented the tracker tag. It's a small, flat, waterproof tracker. It has the capability of tracking sharks by satellite many years after the shark is released. On a trip to the National Aquarium, I was given a handful of those tracker tags and was told that if I ever caught a shark, to tag it and they could track it. So out I went, trying to catch a shark, and you know what? I caught one. A Nurser shark. So we tagged it and the biologists taught me how to upload the number into my cell phone. The shark must've died a few years later cause I lost track of him, but anyway, that's how I found you. I put about five of them in your shoes, way back before you were kidnapped .... the first time."

"But I thought, at the warehouse you said that you were the master mind?" she asked, confused.

"Well, yes and no. I did originally plan it, but I was helped to change my mind about doing it by God and a guy named Jeb."

"Jeb who? Jeb Jensen?"

"Yeah, you know him?"

"Yes, he used to visit our house and leave magazines every weekend. He's a good person from what I can remember."

"Yeah," Micah continued, "he really was. He died not long after that …." he recalled mournfully.

"Sorry."

"Until him, I hadn't seen anyone in authority act with a sense of justice or morality. He was the first person I'd met who seemed to have the answers. Up until then I had felt like a constant victim of the world and of my circumstances. You know, I was living in a 'nothing for free …. if you're not cheating, you're not trying,' type of world."

"I know what you mean," she sympathized, "but how is kidnapping an innocent girl a solution to that problem? I mean, that's just victimizing someone else?"

"No, you're right. Jeb was right. That's why I decided not to do it. And that's why I tried to convince them to leave you alone. But when it became apparent that they were determined, I felt my only recourse was to stop them or save you, one of the two. I never intended to hurt you, if that's any consolation."

"It's not."

"I suppose saying I'm sorry wouldn't work either?"

"Probably not," she said, turning to face him, putting a cold hand on his cheek.

"But I brought you a puppy," he said, smiling.

"Nope. Still no good," she whispered, squeezing him.

"Your ring is cold, wife," he whispered, kissing her shoulder.

"Not consummated."

"We'll have to change that."

"Still don't forgive you," she challenged, stubbornly.

"*No?*"

"No ...." She whispered, kissing him.

CHAPTER 38

THE PLAN

She filled him in on her plan early the next morning. It was an audacious plan, but somehow there seemed to be no other option. So it was decided that they would have to work together if they even hoped to have a chance.

The truth was though, he had serious misgivings about shooting Yak. He had accidentally done it before and it was one of those type sins that he was still trying to get over.

Vividly, he still remembered the day after the shooting. He thought back to the day it all finally sunk in. He was fifteen years old, still it had been enough. Simply enough. To breathe another breath, to live another day, just wasn't worth it at that time. Not anymore. It had been enough.

Enough travels, enough big takes, enough skin tight escapes. But he couldn't, wouldn't escape that time, didn't want to.

That time the man chasing him couldn't be outrun, couldn't be out-foxed, couldn't even be talked down.

After all, it was him. And he was calling it a day, a year, a life. It was over then, and somehow there was a relief to it since it had been decided upon. It had been enough. This is what he told Mike as he sat in his living room after watching the breaking news. The news that he had just killed a man, an innocent man, the night before.

Deprived children of their father, the world of a good man. And though Micah knew the shot that had killed him had been an accident, still it had been enough.

Mike Emerson who had been his home base, his best friend, his listening ear, listened to his last words. Instructions of a soon to be dead man. Mike knew instinctively, that there was no talking him out of it. After all, he was nothing if not a man of his word. A man who did whatever it was he set out to do.

Micah had told him to call the police in a few hours. Explain that it was him and that it had been an accident.

There was no need to pursue him, as he would pursue himself to his end.

For the first time he would be chased down with success. And so he smoked his last bowl of weed in silence with his best friend and then said good-bye.

The lake where he had thrown the gun sometime after midnight the night before was Lake Union. A serene and peaceful lake located near the center of downtown Seattle. That is where his life would all finally, mercifully, come to an end.

As the bus dropped him off he had the acute awareness that he was taking his last few steps. He began to think of the black silence that only death can bring.

He knew it wouldn't hurt much and that was of some comfort to him as he wanted the simple peace of death. The silence of it.

He had stood there at the waterside peering into the depths, as somewhere beneath the small wooden dock laid the chrome .357. The sun shone brilliantly as if saying good-bye in the perfect send off. He'd thought of how it was going to be a waste of a perfectly good day as he dove, fully clothed, beneath the dock. On the first try he came up empty. Too deep. The second try was better as, with more effort, he felt the cold steel of the barrel, but was too short of breath to get a full grip before coming back up for air. The third time took all the strength he had left but eventually he pulled it up from the murky deep. So that was it. Up to his chest in water without a soul to witness his anonymous exit. He remembered wondering how long it would be before they found his body, if they found it at all. He mouthed wordlessly his final apology to God for his existence and raised the muzzle to his temple.

He pulled the trigger. 'Click.' The gun didn't go off! At first he thought it was because it was too wet, but upon examination found that somehow he had emptied it of bullets the night before. How could he have forgotten that? That is where his history changed. That is where somehow he had gone from a casualty, the second as a result of the same incident, to a survivor. But more than a survivor.

In the time it would take him to go home to retrieve the bullets, he would change. He would decide to live. But to live he would have to run.

To run faster and farther than he had ever run before. He'd traveled from city to city, state to state, avoiding the police but was being torn up from the inside out.

He just couldn't forgive himself.

Months later, when he was caught, he'd felt relieved.

And when the sentence was handed down he'd felt as though maybe the pain would go away.

But it didn't. Instead, he became angry at everyone, including himself. True, he'd wanted revenge against the Prosecutor, but that had nothing to do with the way he felt about the loss of life itself.

It had been senseless. And he knew it.

Just like Casey's new plan.

She was determined and didn't seem open to discussion about it, at this point anyway. Still, she was in her element. She knew the area, the cabin and the terrain. Plus, it was her mother whose life was at stake.

She seemed completely prepared for the cold weather, and had packed enough clothes and food for a month long stakeout. Course, she is a woman, he thought to himself, and they never pack light. Yet in this particular circumstance it was a lifesaver for them both as he had brought nothing in advance.

"What are you thinking?" she asked as they laid on their stomachs at the edge of the cliff peering through the scope at the cabin below.

"I'm thinking I should've dressed warmer," he replied, covering over his deeper concerns.

She scooted closer to him, wrapping an arm around him.

"Better?"

"Much," he said, leaning over, gently kissing her on the forehead.

"So what are you *really* thinking?" She had always had a way of cutting to his core, knowing his body language.

"You mean besides waiting to take a shot at the Abominable Snowman, hoping he simply drops like a stone instead of running back into the cabin and stockading himself in there with your mother, like a wounded lion? You mean besides that?"

"Yeah, besides that," she chuckled.

"Nothing," he paused for a bit, wondering if she was willing to consider other options.

"Ok, so what's your plan ... husband?" she asked sincerely, staring into his eyes.

"Well, I was thinking .... I think that Yak is using a handheld scanner," he answered contemplatively.

"Ok ... so?" "So .... Handheld scanners pick up only local police transmissions."

"Ok. And that helps us how?"

"Well, if we were to say, call the police back in say, Seattle, then there is no way he could pick up their communication from this far away. We just tell the police about the scanner he's using and warn them to go radio silent in this area."

"Ok. So let's say we call the police now, from your cell phone ….. is it possible that Yak could pick up that call on his scanner? You know, the cell phone call."

"Uh, I don't think so ….." he paused uncertainly.

"Um, you don't think so? Or you know for a fact, my husband. Cause, that's my mother down there and we need to KNOW so," she emphasized.

"Well, when you put it that way, I don't know for an absolute certainty. So if we're going to do this, then we'll need a land line."

"Well, where is the nearest land line" she asked.

"McDonald's I think. I stopped by there before I found you."

"You left the food in the car right? Meaning, you didn't bring McDonald's into a hungry forest in the dead of winter, did you?" she asked, peering at him accusingly. She didn't need to go any farther, as his silence on the subject gave him away.

"So where are you parked?" he asked, changing the subject.

"Can't use my car."

"Why not?"

"No chains."

"Tell me you didn't come all the way out to a HUNGRY FOREST in the middle of winter without snow chains?" He was on a roll now.

"Where's your Jeep Micah?" she asked, changing the subject.

"Ooooh, so we're back to proper names, huh? My Jeep is down there," he said, pointing to the snow covered road just past the cabin.

"*Great.*" She complained. "So the plan is, I climb down there, cross the river …. *again*, sneak past the cabin, get into your Jeep, find McDonald's and call the police? Am I getting this right?"

"Yeah, and remember to tell them to go radio silent for at least 50 miles or so of this place. What? Wait a minute! Why are you going and not me?" he asked, finally catching on to her twist.

"Because, my love, you can shoot him. You've done it before, right?"

"Hey, that was an accident! I told you about that," he objected.

"I know babe, but I'm just saying you'd be a better shot than me. I've never even pulled a trigger before. Besides one of us has to stay. Because if the police somehow do make a mistake and use their radios, Yak could simply leave and take my mother with him. Then where would we be?"

"Ok, wife. But what if he comes out while you're passing by, and I miss? What then? What's plan C?"

"Plan C, my husband, is pray before you take the shot. Maybe he'll go down like Goliath."

CHAPTER 39

ABOMINABLE SNOWMAN

She stood up from the cliffs edge abruptly and grabbed the descent rope, preparing to leave.

"Wait a minute!" He grabbed her arm, delaying her.

"What?" she asked, teasing.

"Uh …. did I miss the 'on your mark, get set' …. part?" he asked, raising an eyebrow.

"Oh, well, I guess, 'if you're not cheating, you're not trying. Right?" she laughed, pulling him in for a kiss.

"Yeah, well, careful with that first step, wife," he said, hugging her.

"What?" she turned to Mini, who was nipping her pant leg. "Don't worry, I'll be right back."

And with that she began her descent. Noticeably, the ground felt much colder now, without her. He ignored it and laid back down, training an eye through the gun scope. A few tense moments passed before she emerged into view below, sprinting out into the open towards the river. She was right, he thought to himself. Sin is sometimes described as nothing more than simply missing the mark. But this time he couldn't afford to miss. He said a silent prayer and lined up the cross-hairs on the cabin below.

She emerged from the tree line, near the cabin and unexpectedly sprinted the distance of the clearing to the cabin, crouching under its eaves.

"What are you doing, babe?" he whispered nervously. "Go around babe, around it. Not *to* it."

He watched in horror as she crept up under the window, taking a peek inside.

"What are you doing Casey?" he felt helpless as he watched.

Seemingly satisfied, she rounded the cabin for the other side, disappearing from his view temporarily. He waited anxiously for her to reappear, but as the moments passed by he began to have that sinking feeling in his stomach. Something had gone wrong, he knew it. She should've emerged a long time ago and headed to the Jeep. But as the moments ticked past, he knew it was time to go.

"Well, Mini? Ready to get back in the backpack?" he asked the eager dog, expressly dying for action.

"ANGEL!!! ANGEL!!!" Suddenly he heard her screaming down below, somewhere in front of the cabin. He took a look through the scope. Nothing. Mini barked up at him, sensing his mood change. "Yup, time to go get mom. In the pack girl." He scooped up Mini and grabbed the rope, descending so quickly that by ropes' end he had burned both hands.

Taking off at a dead run he headed straight into her previous footsteps, following them across the river and into the tree line. He paused there for a moment to take in the scene. "Still nothing Mini," he whispered as he broke from the tree line out into the expanse, finally arriving around the front of the cabin.

He came to a stop in confusion. Just ten feet from the front porch, blood stained the snow in a spray pattern with footprints that struck out in all directions. He stepped backward …. a step that he immediately regretted.

SNAP!!!!!!

"Ugggh!!! Ahhhg!!!" Micah writhed in pain, buckling to the ground. Swinging blindly at the wolf on his leg, screaming. "DOWN! DOWN BOY!!!" But it wasn't working. In fact, the wolf began biting down harder as Micah shut his eyes trying to handle the pain. He swiped wildly at it again and again, eventually striking it. No fur? He thought as he felt not fur but rather … steel. It was metal.

"Monin boss. Comfy? Cozy? Now yall didn't just thank yall was gonna walk up on me with no problem was ya? That there boss is a bonafide antique. They don't make bear traps like dat no mo. Somethin' bout it bein inhumane. Inhumane for a bear. Dat make sense to you, boss?" Micah sunk down in despair, looking at his leg now gushing with blood. Looking around, there was the gun. A few feet away. Must have dropped it during the bite.

"I wouldn't try it boss," Yak said, going into the house and re-appearing with Sheila, being grabbed by the hair.

"SAY IT!" he demanded, shaking her head. She whimpered, but eventually screamed, "ANGEL ... ANGEL!"

"See dat there? Uncanny ain't it? She sound just like Casey, don she?" he asked, proud of his cunning.

Micah clenched his teeth, seething in pain, as things began to cloud up in his head, making it difficult to plan a way out of it.

"What do you want Yak?" he asked, feeling out of options.

"Oh, now yall wanna play nice, huh? Is this how yall treat family?" he asked innocently, pulling up his shirt to reveal a fresh stab wound.

"YOU STABBED ME MAMA!!!" he screamed out to the tree line.

She done stabbed me again wid this thang!" he said, disappointed, pulling out the butterfly knife.

Micah was surprised to see it again, but was in too much pain to register the implications of it all.

"NA YOU COME OUTTA THEM THERE WOODS, MAMA! I GOT YO HUSBAND AND I GOT YO MA. YOU REMEMBER DA DINOSAURS? NA YOU COME OUT!" His voice bellowed in the now conspicuously quiet forest.

Casey emerged from the tree line, dejected and defeated.

"No Casey!" Micah protested. But it was pointless. Her body language alone made it clear.

"For better or for worse." She declared, as she walked up to Yak.

She climbed up the porch steps and gave him her hands as he cuffed them. "I just got one last request Yak," she said, now resigned to her fate.

"What you want mama?" he asked, suddenly a small child again.

"You let him and her go and I'll go with you, be your mama. But first let me take that thing off of him, ok? He can't do anything to you now, he's got a broken leg. Let me go and say good-bye," she implored him, taking his large hand in hers.

Yak took a look at Micah. Finally satisfied. "Yeah, you go on head. Take her too," he said, releasing Sheila.

Casey and Sheila came walking over to Micah as he struggled to open the jaws of the device.

"Let us help you with that," Casey said as she and her mother opened up the jaws and helped Micah back to his feet, leaning upon Sheila for support.

"So, um. Just wanted to use one at this point," she said, rubbing the tears from his eyes and brushing back some hair from his face.

"Use what?" he asked sorrowfully.

"An 'I told you so'," she said, braving a smile.

"You sure you want to use one now? We're going to be married forever, and you only get ten 'I told you so's.' You sure? You're going to be down to nine left," he smiled through the pain.

"Yup. I think the moment calls for it. My plan was better than yours. I told you so," she whispered, kissing his cheek.

"You know what I'm most afraid of babe?"

"What my husband?"

"Nothing," he said, using the last of his strength to stand erect, grabbing her around the waist while pulling her in for a deep kiss.

"ALL RIGHT NOW!!! YALL DONE SAID YO GOODBYE. NA GO INSIDE MA!" Yak demanded, as Casey turned and went in with him.

Micah and Sheila struggled back to the base of the cliff. At the ropes, he began strapping the backpack onto her, then the climbing harness that he'd left behind on his descent.

He would have to free climb, he knew. Hand over hand, as his legs were now all but useless. And it was just as well as he never did get to the lesson on how to properly use leg gripping.

"CLIMB MICAH!!! CLIMB!!!" Somehow, Casey came running for her life out of the clearing, Yak trailing behind.

Yak was strong, but all of that muscle made him heavier. A disadvantage in the deep snow. While Casey was nearly leaping with each step, Yak seemed to fall deeper with each renewed effort, expanding the distance between them.

In a moment that seemed to happen in slow motion, Casey finally reached the rope, her mother clearing the top. "CLIMB MICAH!" She demanded, attempting to lift him up as he struggled.

"No. You go first." He corrected her, knowing it was her Yak was after. Taking a look back, Yak was still a little ways off but closing quickly. She took one look into his eyes and knew there simply wasn't time to argue.

With that, she began to climb, Micah pulling up the rear.

He was nearly halfway up the rope and could already hear Casey's voice as she spoke on the phone to the police. They were going to make it! He, was going to make …. suddenly he felt the rope tighten beneath him.

Yak.

Yak's superior upper body strength was now becoming an advantage, as he quickly ascended the rope at twice the speed Micah had been going. Looking back, Micah realized the cold truth of the matter. Yak would soon overtake him, and with him …. Casey.

Pausing, he looked up into her waiting eyes, as she was now desperately pulling on the rope. "Did I ever tell you that I love you?" he asked her as she began desperately reaching out for him.

"No baby! Don't give up! PLEASE ...." she called back tearfully.

"Well Casey, I love you. Always have." He pulled out his favorite multi-tool from his shirt pocket. *"Never know when it'll come in handy"* he whispered to himself. And with one fluid motion cut the rope.

CHAPTER 40

SUPERIOR COURT

IN THE SUPERIOR COURT OF THE
STATE OF WASHINGTON
AND IN THE COUNTY OF KING

STATE OF WASHINGTON, NO. 79-8-4-87

    PLAINTIFF

    VS

TATE, MICAH, DEFENDANT

COMES NOW the Prosecuting Attorney of KING COUNTY and for the STATE OF WASHINGTON hereby charges the Defendant with the following crimes:

COUNT I:	KIDNAPPING IN THE FIRST DEGREE RCW 9A.40.020
COUNT 11:	CRIMINAL MISTREATMENT FIRST DEGREE RCW 9A.42.02
COUNT III:	UNLAWFUL POSSESSION OF A FIREARM RCW 9A.41.040
COUNT IV:	INTERFERING WITH A CRIMINAL INVESTIGATION RCW 9A.36

WRITE:

The State does allege that Defendant Tate did willfully and knowingly kidnap one Casey Law along with four others within the State of Washington and in the jurisdiction of the County of King.

The State does also allege that Defendant Tate did also kidnap one Casey Law a second time outside of Washington jurisdiction along with one Johnson Jones (a.k.a. "Yak"), fugitive of Washington State Justice Department. This latter information provided to attest that Defendant did in fact have knowledge of Johnson and did aid Johnson, a known fugitive.

Although the victim denies these allegations, the State approved psychiatrist and leading medical expert, has found Mrs. Tate to be legally insane. This by means of extensive "brainwashing" by the same Defendant Tate. Which "brainwashing" Defendant achieved by way of multiple stalker type moves, by which he disabled Mrs. Tate's clear thinking faculties. To said "brainwashing", the State has ample proof by means of multiple exhibits, not the least of which Exhibit A: Casey's Diary, wherein she herself freely admits to "brainwashing", and being 'crazy.'

This evidence is undeniable proof that Mrs. Tate's testimony should be disallowed from public record, nor taken into account in these proceedings. The State does also charge that the marriage between Casey Law and Micah Tate should be considered unlawful due to such previous mentioned "brainwashing", and as such she was in no condition to enter into a legal contract. It is therefore this Prosecutor's opinion that the witness Mrs. Tate should be treated as single and therefore no longer covered by the Constitutional Rights of a spouse, as it relates to direct cross-examination.

As to the final matter under consideration. The State does acknowledge that the accused is unable to physically attend at trial, due to his 'condition' as stated by the doctors at Swedish Hospital.

That said 'condition' being a 'deep coma.' However, the State believes that the defendant is in fact faking said 'coma' in order to avoid prosecution. The State would ask the court to take into consideration that the Defendant has been tested as a 'rare genius' and is therefore fully capable of such trickery. Further, the Prosecutor's office has brought in its own 'expert,' the aforementioned psychiatrist, who, after independently examining Defendant Tate, found his brain wave patterns to be completely within 'normal standards.' She even said he was quote "seemingly alert." Her explanation is as follows:

Defendant Tate does exhibit all symptoms common to the diagnosis of a coma as the Doctors have suggested. However, there is every reason to believe that he is in fact awake and fully conscious.

It is true that his heart rate and other vitals are at dangerous lows for which he is currently on a respirator.

However, these very same symptoms can readily be found in Eastern lands among the Tibetan Monks.

The practice is called 'Controlled Chi,' 'Russian Wind,' or 'Flying Monk,' all of which is the practice of mind over body in order to achieve inner-peace or some other altruistic goal.

In short, the Monk enters a deep meditative state allowing him to transcend normal human limits and pressures such as cold, heat or pain.

The state begins with controlled breathing, slowing down one's pulse while simultaneously feeding the blood supply extraordinary amounts of oxygen causing dilation of pupils and a higher body temperature, the same as a bear does in hibernation. Because the Monk remains motionless, very little energy or sustenance is necessary. Tibetan Monks have been known to endure extreme exposure in sub-zero temperatures, or scorching heat, for many months at a time as a rite of passage.

In such a state, many Western doctors would assume the patient to be a victim of a coma. All symptoms being equal except for one. Brain waves.

While a person in a deep coma usually shows little or no brain activity, the Tibetan Monk's brain is fully active.

I have examined Micah Tate and fully believe him to be aware and awake, even if his vitals would suggest otherwise.

END DEPOSITION.

These aforementioned facts taken into account, the State asks this Court to proceed with the trial in absence of Defendant Tate, as his guilt is quite obvious considering the following evidences, should it please the Court to note. Such evidence is as follows:

1) Duct tape, found in the warehouse (original scene) had Defendant Tate's fingerprints imprinted on it.

2) Blood particles found on a rosebush fence, outside of Ms. Law's window is a confirmed match to the DNA sample taken from Tate.

3) Numbered 'Shark style' tracking devices were found in Ms. Law's shoes. The trackers were matched on file to trackers given to Defendant Tate at National Aquarium of Guam.

4) Testimony of Johnson Jones, A.K.A. "Yak" postmortem. In which Johnson also testifies that he and the Defendant Tate, were 'Family' and 'Brothers,' in one of his poems found at the St. Helen's cabin after Johnson's body was discovered at the bottom of a cliff in this same area. It became immediately apparent to crime scene investigators that Johnson was clearly trying to rescue Defendant Tate.

5) Night vision goggles found at the scene in Santa Barbara laden with 'Yak's' fingerprints and traced back to Radio Shack, is solid physical evidence that supports the connection and plan developed between the two of them while Defendant Tate worked at Radio Shack

Such evidence testifies to the closeness between the Defendant Tate and the known fugitive 'Yak.'

These things taken into consideration, the State Prosecutor is asking for Life without Parole for Defendant Tate.

SUPREME COURT IN THE STATE OF WASHINGTON

DECISION: This Court does find that the evidence against Tate is formidable.

As to the marital status of Mrs. Tate: the ceremony and license were obtained in the State of California and it is therefore not within the jurisdiction of this Court to decide on such things. She will be granted marital status and with it therefore all constitutional rights it carries.

This Court is concerned as to the health status of the Defendant, however, it finds that there exists sufficient evidence to suggest that the Defendant is capable, should he care to, to join these proceedings. Thus the Court finds reason to proceed with trial in absence of Defendant.

PROCEED: Trial date has been set.

CHAPTER 41
CASEY'S NEW DIARY
ENTRY 1

Dear diary,

The Bible says to honor your father and your mother. But my father, the Governor, is forcing a trial through against my husband. My mother, today, cracked up on the witness stand while being asked questions from the Defense attorney. Mind you, these weren't questions from the Prosecution. So I can only imagine how tomorrow's testimony will go upon cross examination.

I mean, I love my father. But we have definitely lost something between us. That old lady has him under her psychiatric spell. She's now his main advisor and the Prosecutors 'medical expert.'

I did some research of my own and found that she used to work for a 'Psychic Hotline' before she landed this job.

So my theory is that Susan Bower. a.k.a. 'old hag,' was called just after my original kidnapping. My father, wanting a psychiatrist for his disturbed daughter, in his desperation, accidentally called for a psychic instead of a psychiatrist and offered a large sum of money for an emergency intervention. Susan Bower, a struggling glorified telemarketer saw the opportunity and seized it. From what I could tell, she had no actual degrees or formal training as a psychiatrist. She then brilliantly weaved a story of my Angel being 'imaginary.' She was accustomed to weaving stories over the phone, so this actually came natural to her and served her purposes. Because, if in fact Angel was real, then I had no psychological problems and thus she was once again out of a lucrative job. But if she could convince my father that my problems were deep and would need extra sessions, well then it was perfect for her.

Somehow the police also assumed she was a real doctor given that she was chosen by the powerful politician himself. One thing led to another and now here she is the 'medical expert.' I told Micah's attorneys about my discoveries regarding Susan Bower, but they passed it off as the "ravings of a desperate but delusional wife of the accused."

I'm sitting here at the foot of my husband's bed, as I have every day for two weeks now. I get flashbacks in my dreams of him cutting that rope. Over and over it re-plays in my mind. I keep wondering if I could've convinced him out of it, or maybe if I would've just reached a little farther, maybe I could've grabbed him.

Yak landed first, dying instantly. Micah landed partially on top of him, sparing him the majority of the impact. Nevertheless, he still hit his head on some rocks on the way down. The doctors say he has less than a twenty percent chance of ever waking up. They say that even if he does wake up he's likely to have lost all memory. Not only the memory of me, but also the memory of how to walk and talk. They say it may not be worth the effort, or cost. I cannot bear to tell you how many people have asked me to think about taking him off of life support. Even well-meaning friends have asked me to 'seriously' consider it. But he made a promise to me once and I for one believe that nothing is impossible for God or for him. He has proven to me over and over again that he can, and will, do the impossible, so I figure what's one more miracle.

The trial is a farce. A lie. A set-up. A scandal. My dad doesn't just want my husband to go to prison. No, that's not even close to his aim. Dad wants him dead. He honestly believes that my husband was collaborating with Yak and that I am just naïve as to what was "really going on," but as I said, the trial is all a set-up.

You see, if my husband is found guilty, then he will become a 'Ward of the State of Washington.' That being the case, the State would become ultimately responsible for his health care, IE: they can and will take him off of life support, effectively killing him. All they would need to do this is a signature. A signature of none other than the Governor of Washington State.

So …. my husband is literally on trial for his life. Defenseless and unable to testify, they are pushing ahead with it, using trickery and lies, most of which are coming out of the mouth of one 'old hag.'

In other news. Each day, two mail men arrive at the hospital with mail for us. Two full bags of it. I had no idea that so many people were interested in our story. I have read maybe a hundred or so of these letters to him. Most of them late into the night while waiting for him to come back to me. Letters entitled: "Save Angel," and "Casey Fan." Some of it is pretty strange and others touch my heart.

In the media, many of the facts get all twisted up and people take that idea into their minds and take it another step further, until it becomes a totally different story altogether. But they mean well, I know. Online, there's even a "Casey and Angel Fan" web site. I don't know who set it up or who is organizing it but I am so thankful, because so many donations have come in that I can keep my husband alive indefinitely .... if he wins.

Every day, hundreds of people rush up the steps of City Hall and pack the courtroom, hoping to get a glimpse of what has become the most intriguing trial of the greater Seattle area. People bring signs and posters with pictures of him. Yesterday I even saw a little girl wearing a T-shirt that read, "Save the Angels, God is Watching."

So that's how these last two weeks have been for us, as I keep him updated every night, knowing at some point soon he will wake up with all of the answers, just like he always does. During the day I am at the trial and at night I am with him.

Occasionally, the friends sneak in Mini to see him but the doctors get pretty upset, so mostly it's just him and me. I don't want to be away from him even for a moment. It's not like I'm there to testify or anything as they have deemed me 'unstable.' But I go because I don't want it to look like I am not in full support of him. The public's eye may not be the most important concern, but I've learned how public opinion can sway important decisions. I am after all, a politician's daughter. And right now my husband and I need the public, as it seems they and God are the only ones we have left on our side. To that end I pray continuously, day and night, that we will win, that he will wake up, that he will remember me.

But the fact is that it all seems to be going the other way. The evidence continues to pour in from the Prosecutors office, seemingly proving him guilty. But to me, every detail about where he was and what he did for me is further proof of his love. Not just his love for me but also his love for God.

When the doctors gave me his personal effects that first night when he was admitted into their care I found a small article in his back pocket entitled, "Questions from Readers." The question under discussion was, "Does a person, newly baptized but having formally committed crimes, have to turn himself in to the police for crimes committed prior to learning the Bible's standards?"

The answer was surprising to me I'll admit. It pointed out that in the first century, many who became Christians were once formerly criminals, 1 Corinthians 6: 11. And yet they were not told to turn themselves in to the Romans or the priests after baptism. Further, Paul himself harbored a fugitive (Onesimus) for many months while teaching him Bible truths. The article therefore concluded that it was a matter of conscience but a newly baptized person is not biblically bound to turn himself in. Yet, if the person had done something in the past that continues to constitute an "ongoing trauma or crime" to a person or persons, then, in that case, the "offender was under obligation by the law of Christ (love neighbor as self) to try to correct the wrong to the extent that it was still humanly possible."

That article helped me greatly to understand his thinking. I have carried it ever since, everywhere I go. That and the handcuff key he secretly passed into my mouth with that final kiss in the snow. He was there in that bear trap barely holding himself together, when he whispered "you know what I'm most afraid of?" A question that seemed out of place given the moment, until I remembered his proposal. Then I knew what he'd meant and it was confirmed when I felt the key enter my mouth.

Tomorrow is the big day. The last day of testimony, closing arguments and maybe even the verdict if the jury is satisfied. It all hinges on my mother's cross-examination, if she can prove that Yak kidnapped her, that he was in fact crazy …. then maybe the court will believe her, change their view of Yak's poem and thus exonerate my husband. Still, even though I know that this is the most important day of the trial, I'm going to stay right here with him. We started this together and we are going to watch our fate on TV .... together.

I'm with him now as I write this. He's lying there so calm, so peacefully, with that ethereal look of contentment on his face. I can't help but think of the angels in heaven and how content they must feel being so close to someone who has all the answers. Well .... If you're listening to me now God, I have one last request to make. Once, I learned that baby ducklings will forever love the first living being they see upon coming out of their shells.

Well .... Let my husband see me first when he awakens .... I'll be waiting. In the name of your son, Christ Jesus, Amen.

CHAPTER 42

THE VERDICT

Casey sat at the end of Micah's hospital bed biting her fingernails and occasionally pacing the floor, as the Prosecution laid into her mother upon cross-examination.

PROSECUTOR: "So, you say Yak *kidnapped* you against your will, correct?"
WITNESS: "Yes." (crying)
PROSECUTOR: "But you admit that you had spoken to him several times before the cabin incident, correct?"
WITNESS: "Yes, he bought me a drink or two once. Back before the wedding. At the time, he seemed like a nice man.

The Prosecutor stares at her sarcastically while directing the jury's attention to the blown up photo of Yak. Drawing some looks of dis-belief among them.
PROSECUTOR: "In fact, you thought he was more than just a "nice man." Did you not in fact, have sexual relations with Yak?"

WITNESS: I wasn't in my right mind. He probably put something in my drink!" Prosecutor addresses the Judge: "Your Honor, the State asks that that last statement be stricken from the record, as the witness is not a medical expert and therefore cannot rightly testify to having been 'drugged.'

JUDGE: "The jury will disregard the witness' comment of 'being drugged.'

PROSECUTOR: But you did have sex with him willfully, correct?"

WITNESS: "I guess so ...... I don't know. It's hazy."

PROSECUTOR: "It's hazy? Did you not in fact invite Yak to your daughter's wedding thereafter?"

WITNESS: "Well, yes. But ...."

PROSECUTOR: "And after the wedding. You didn't notice your daughter was missing for 3 days?"

WITNESS: "She was newly married! Everyone is missing for at least 3 days afterward probably, except for YOU!"

Courtroom breaks out in muted laughter. Judge bangs gavel ordering: "Order in the courtroom!"

PROSECUTOR: "Very funny. But this is quite serious! And my point is that you didn't at all suspect foul play, even though you now claim Yak to be a violent person and 'dangerous.' And yet as dangerous as you say he was, you were totally un-concerned about your missing daughter. Is that correct?"

WITNESS: "But that was before the cabin ......"

PROSECUTOR: "Thank you for bringing up the cabin. I have one last question to ask the witness before the State rests its case. Remember Sheila, you are under oath."

WITNESS: "Yes, I know."

PROSECUTOR: "In that case, tell the jury the truth. You were not even handcuffed on your way to Mt. St. Helen's. You could have in fact, jumped out of the car at any moment! Is that not correct?"

WITNESS: "Yes ... but ... I was afraid!"

PROSECUTOR: "Afraid of a man whom you had slept with? Whom you had invited to the wedding? Whom you later willfully rode along with to Mt. St. Helen's? No! You weren't afraid were you? No, but rather, you shared Yak's vision didn't you? You wanted a family again! A family you had squandered away through drugs and alcohol! You agreed with Yak and the Defendant Tate! And you even wrote a letter to entrap your own daughter into coming down there, didn't you?"

WITNESS: "NO! IT WASN'T LIKE THAT!!!"

PROSECUTOR: "I have no further questions for this so called witness. The State rests!"

The courtroom buzzed with anticipation and rumors as the jury left the courtroom to deliberate.

Casey sat nervously as armed guards entered into the privacy of their hospital room, awaiting the verdict.

The jury began re-entering the courtroom as Casey sent up a silent prayer, including just one word. "Please."

JUDGE: "Has the jury come to a verdict?

JURY FOREMAN: "Yes."

JUDGE: "Is the verdict unanimous?"

JURY FOREMAN: "Yes."

JUDGE: "Will the Defense team please rise for the reading of the verdict. But I want to warn this courtroom, that when the verdict is read there will be no outbursts or demonstrations of any kind. Is that clear? Fine. Then Jury Foreman, will you please read the verdict."

JURY FOREMAN: "We the jury, as to the first count of kidnapping, we do hereby find the defendant ….. GUILTY as charged."

"As to the second additional charge of Criminal Mistreatment, we do hereby find the defendant ….. GUILTY as charged."

"As to the third charge of Interfering with an Investigation, we do hereby find the defendant ..... GUILTY as charged."

"As to the fourth and final charge of Unlawful Possession of a Firearm, we do hereby find the defendant ..... GUILTY as charged."

Casey screamed at hearing the verdict and flung herself onto the bed, clinging to his chest while the guards attempted to wrestle her away from him, finally breaking her free, hand-cuffing his still unmoving body to the bed railing.

Moments later while her friends and family rushed into the room to support her, she uttered one final word, barely audible ... "No," collapsing.

CHAPTER 43
CASEY'S DIARY ENTRY: LAST

Dear diary,

I really wanted to thank everyone who had helped us, honestly I did. But at this moment, I just can't bring myself to face anyone or even leave my room for that matter. But maybe someone, someday, will read this account. For them, I want to say that life is often filled with forces determined to mold you into doing their will. In my life I have met many such forces. Sometimes they were people, sometimes they were ideas. Yet, all such forces claim to have the answers. There are those who believe re-incarnation is the answer, others believe the world can be saved through politics. The psychiatrist lady believed that science would eventually save all. And my mother, up until now, had simply decided to drown out the problem believing there is no solution.

But I believe I have come to know the best answer for my life. And that answer is love. And God is love. But how can one know God? Well, I believe it could be summed up with the conversation I had with mom that night of the verdict. She asked, "What would move anyone to sacrifice their life like that, as he did for you?" The answer to that question is simple and yet so profound and can be found in the Bible. She now studies these things with me and has given up drinking.

I sat there in that hospital room all day, hoping something would change. That the jury would file back into the courtroom and say, 'it was all a mistake, we take it back' but that never happened of course and now my husband has less than 48 hours to live.

I tried everything I could think of. Called every lawyer who would answer my call. Talked to my father until I lost my voice. All to no end. So, in our last hours together, I want to have it clear in mind what I want to say to him, so I'm writing it down, here in my diary. I want to say: "To my dear husband who taught me so much, about sacrifice, about love, about forgiveness. I now know why Jesus pardoned that man just before he died. I know how he must've felt as he did it. I too want to say, now, what I should have said in that cave. And that is, that I forgive you Micah from the bottom of my heart ….. I forgive you forever. You taught me what it meant to win, to truly win.

And that sometimes, in some situations, just surviving is winning.

And that sometimes winning means temporarily losing, something or someone you love very much. But most of all, I learned that winning is not about how you began the race, but it's about how you are remembered after it's done. And I, and millions like me, will always remember you, not just for who you were or for what you did, but more so for who you became, to yourself, to God, to me. You may not have been a real angel, but you were irrefutably my angel.

I promise that after you go I will wait to see you again, someday, somehow. I don't know how it will be in paradise but I will wait all the same.

And there's one more thing I want to say to you before you go. Something I should've said long ago when we first met. 'Thank you.'

CHAPTER 44

GOODBYES

14 hours left: Casey sat on her bed, disconsolate and motionless. Accepting no calls, ignoring the knocks on her apartment door and closing her eyes even to the light that dared to shine in her darkest hour.

Having been denied one final visit with her husband, she just wanted to be alone. Bereaved of hope and exasperated of optimism, grief-stricken, there just wasn't word enough to describe the agony she felt. Nor could loneliness describe the immeasurable breach left in her heart.

He was being held in a secured room at Swedish Hospital in downtown Seattle. Having been moved from the State Penitentiary in Walla Walla as the prison officials did not want a full scale riot to break out among the population as his story had permeated even the darkest prison cells. Giving hope to some, purpose to others. But mainly a profound sense of injustice among the population.

As the hours clicked by, she found herself sifting listlessly through the letters that had poured in, now strewn about her room and bed. So many people had prayed and as a result had their faith disappointed. Their belief in justice, hope, even God, shaken, even stricken. She knew there was a bigger issue that God was attending to, yet she couldn't help but feel as though this man, her man, had merited special consideration, a second chance, at life, at love.

She closed her eyes and wandered back to her last meaningful conversation with him in the cave that morning after she had fallen through the ice. She laid on him, curled up, enjoying the peaceful rise and fall of his chest.

"Did you ever just want to quit? Just give up on it all?" she asked.

He turned into her arms meeting her eyes. "I did once.... A long time ago. But I learned something that day that I will never forget. The fact is Casey, that all of us were born imperfect. Short of the finish line that continually pants on ahead of us, evading our grasp. But giving up, loss of hope, retiring to despair, is an option we, you and I, do not have. It is not until our darkest hours that we know how strong we truly are, who we really are. It is the not knowing of these essential facts about ourselves that keeps us from reaching our goals. Having never climbed the mountain before, halfway up we estimate we will run out of energy short of the top. But it is not until reaching the farthest point of success or failure that we truly know how much we have in reserve. You will never know how much gas your tank can hold until you run it empty. But once it is empty, you have not failed, you have not fallen short, you are simply better prepared for your next winning run. And thus your first loss is ultimately your first step towards success.

Most winners usually win only once, yet lose many times over. But all losers are losers because they lost once and then gave up, never to try again. True we may lose, we may die, but we will never, ever give up. If for nothing else than because we are in love. And love, our love Casey, will never fail."

She thought of those words and how they had filled her with confidence and hope back when he'd said it. But now those same words echoed in her mind like gangrene, poisoning her reasoning ability as it waged war with her despair. She was being forced to give up, forced to fall short of the goal, forced to let him die. Yet was reminded that he himself would never give up, never let go. For her part, she wasn't even sure if she would survive his end. Or if rather, the loss itself would stop her heart. She was already beginning to wane and wondered if this is what it felt like for those older couples. Those ones that stay married 50 years, happily, but then once one of the partners died, the other soon mysteriously follows.

1 HOUR LEFT: Turning on the TV, she watched as the crowd of protesters gathered outside Swedish Hospital in a last ditch effort to convince the Governor she knew wouldn't be convinced. Traffic was reportedly backed up for miles down I-5 as more and more people arrived to pay their last respects.

Casey laid back on her pillow, not wanting to hear the countdown any longer, yet unwilling to turn it off.

30 MINUTES: It was like her soul was being stabbed with each tick of the clock. She could literally feel it jabbing her side. As if the knife he'd used to help her were finally paying her one last visit. Still, she thought, it really does feel like something's jabbing me. Rolling onto her side, she discovered the source of the irritation. A package. Hmmm. Another one? She turned it over in her hands, examining it, trying to read the sender's address in the darkened room. It read: 'From Scott, Campaign Manager.'

"Hmmm," she mumbled, "what does he want?" Opening the small box she read the small attached letter: 'To Casey. Sorry I couldn't help you before. But here is the film you asked for. Happy hunting with your cinematography class."

Casey shot up in bed. Fully awake now. How could she have forgotten about the garage cameras? Doesn't matter, she thought, as she fumbled nervously with it, trying to stick the DVD into the suddenly far too small slot with shaky hands.

15 MINUTES: Casey had never learned to drive like that, she was making it up as she went, but as she side-swiped two separate vehicles on the I-5 corridor, she suddenly didn't care what she hit. As long as she got there in time.

Turning south past the University District, she cut across two lanes of traffic, screeching her tires as they struggled to make the tight turn, nearly colliding with an on-coming truck in the process. Seeing traffic ahead, she decided for a short-cut through a strip-mall parking lot but immediately regretted it as the scene unfolded before her.

The mall itself sat upon a raised incline that bordered a main artery road that led to the freeway. As such, many people had the custom of cutting across the parking lot that eventually emptied out onto a side road adjacent to the freeway on-ramp.

Unfortunately for Casey, she wasn't the only one using the clever detour. Pedestrians and vehicles packed the parking lot as she sped up and blared the horn hoping that they would all dive out of the way, sensing the urgency. They didn't.

She didn't see the speed bump until it was too late. Maybe she was airborne for only a fraction of a second, but from her cockpit seat it felt like a lifetime as the engine roared menacingly, having come free from its purchase with the ground. 'SLAM!' *"Yup, that did it."* Casey murmured as the sound of the crashing steel animal served notice to the un-aware that she was coming through, and now!

However, not all seemed to get the point, as evidenced by one old lady slowly pushing her grocery cart into the lot, having just exited the Safeway store.

Casey watched it all happen in slow motion as the cart filled with groceries went airborne having been speared by Casey's front grill.

"*Cabbage?*"

Tomatoes and heads of cabbage hit the windshield with a thud, while a can of tuna cracked the windshield and went spinning over the roof.

The same fate would've been held out for grandma too if it weren't for the bag boy yanking her back by her shawl.

It all happened so quickly that Casey hadn't even had a chance to tap the brakes.

"Sorry," was all that meekly came out as she stepped once more on the gas pedal heading for the exit while trying to avoid any more wandering heads of cabbage.

Coming upon stalled traffic waiting to exit the parking lot, Casey pulled left into the 'entry' lane, attempting to exit past the waiting cars.

"*No.*"

Pulling into the lot from a side street came a white Honda Civic whose driver seemed unaware of the sudden game of chicken she'd just entered into by hopping into Casey's lane.

"*Hang on!*"

Casey wasn't even sure who she was talking to as she pulled farther left back into the lot, punching it as it was far too late for anything other than to simply go for it. The cement parking blocks, designed to stop cars from rolling off of the raised embankment, loomed larger in her windshield as she said a silent prayer and grabbed the wheel, bracing for impact.

The loud crack of the suspension giving way as the front wheels lifted up over the blocks, sounded out like a shotgun going off in Casey's ears followed by the deafening silence of the slight breeze coming through a cracked window and the impending doom of the upcoming impact.

"KAABRACK .... A .... BAM!"

The front fender dug a swath of grass out of a decorated strip separating the sidewalk from the street as Casey's bull bucked and broncoed sideways after falling out of the sky like a scene out of a rodeo where they use cars instead of broncos.

She paid no attention to the close call, hearing his words in her mind. "Focus darling, forget everything around you, like tunnel vision, just focus on your objective."

She ran his words over and over again in her mind while heading into downtown Seattle weaving dangerously past slower traffic.

5 MINUTES: "No! GET OUT OF THE WAY!!!" she screamed, as traffic came to stand-still 3 blocks from the hospital. Abandoning the still running car in traffic, Casey flew down First Avenue on foot, using every ounce of energy she had left to fly. "Fly Casey!

Fly!!" she encouraged herself as she passed the burgeoning crowd in a blur of red hair and determination.

They began cheering as she approached the concentrated center, thinking she was there to lead the rally. Others locked arms before her, creating a corridor of people and clearing a path through to the hospital. "MOVE!!!" someone screamed behind her. Turning, she discovered she was being chased by a mounted officer, apparently there for crowd control. "You want a ride? I can get you there!" he yelled as the crowds split before him. Asking nothing further, she mounted the horse behind him as the crowd began to chant: "GO CASEY, GO!!!"

Arriving, she flung herself down as the charging beast mounted the final steps, four at a time, as though it intended to enter in right along with them.

1 MINUTE: "DAD!!! DAD!!! Don't do it! He's innocent! I can prove it!" she screamed as she came running down the hallway to meet him.

"Honey, you've been through a lot. It's time to let him go now," he said consolingly.

"No dad, this is for real! I have video proof!"

"Honey, court is over, it's too ….."

"Listen to me dad! If you would ever have listened to me in your entire life, then PLEASE listen to me now! Just look at it! You'll see."

Her father, seeing the determination in her eyes, turned to one of his men ordering, "Go ahead, run it on that monitor over there."

The DVD uploaded, the entire fight scene unfolded before them all as the room abruptly grew silent. It looked like a grainy, second rate horror film as blood flew through the air while Yak took his first blow to the face. It seemed impossible but somehow it was all undeniably, shockingly, real.

There he was, Micah, fighting for Casey's life in the dimly lit garage on Tacoma's Hill Top. It was a mismatch of epic proportions. He fought, ducked and rolled away from the menacing blows of the giant attacker, all the while trying to find a way into the van. But he was so small, Casey thought to herself, it almost seemed like it was one of those nature films featuring a badger fighting a bear. He weaved past the blows, desperately trying to wake her from sleep.

The DVD was still playing its gruesome scene as Casey and her father were already running down the hall, eventually bursting into the operating room. "Stop, stop, he can live, he can live!!!" he yelled, slamming open the operating room doors. The doctors jumped back in surprise, but, to Casey, all she noticed was the heart monitor's shrill tone of flat line, her lifeless husband, unmoving on the table.

"No!!!" Casey wailed, jumping onto the bed, ripping off the sensory equipment. "He can't die! It can't end like this!" she protested, maddeningly striking him repeatedly on his chest, begging for any sign of life.

The doctors, helpless, finally turned off the monitor, one of them saying: "I'm sorry, you're too late, we disconnected him five minutes ago." Sinking the room into a cold silence as her father now knew it to be over.

"Turn it back on!" she demanded, striking him again, blowing into his mouth.

Her father nodded slowly to the doctors, who, taking his lead .... silently exited the room.

DO YOU BELIEVE IN ANGELS?

Dry, his throat was so dry. And such blinding light, far too bright for his eyes as they struggled to focus on it. What is it? "Who?"

Casey abruptly woke up with a start from her corner chair. "Did …. Did …. you say something?" she asked, holding her breath.

Such a brilliant cloudy brightness, and fiery red, there, just over there in the corner. Hermosa. Who? What is she? Not human, far too radiant, majestic, almost …. celestial. Ruby. Must be a million rubies in the curls of her hair. Jade .. no … ice. Fiery eyes of luminous jade. An angel? Cherub? "What?" she said, standing up in amazement. "Did you say something?"

"Um …" he stammered, sitting up. "Are you an angel?"

"No, but you are." She stood there wondering if it was a dream, not believing the moment.

"Where … where am I? Is … is this paradise?"

"Seattle." She smiled.

"Hmmm … Seattle? Where's Seattle and who …. What …. are you?"

"I'm Casey." Burning tears began forming in the corners of her eyes as she moved in to embrace him, but stopped short as he put up a hand to stop her.

"Don't. Please. Wait. I'm not ready to go yet. I ... I have things, I'm sure I have something unfinished. Um ... to ...do. Just please ... time ... I just need more time. Who, who am I?" he asked, his face impassive.

"Well, you're my angel, my husband and we, we are in love. You've been asleep for a month, my love. You almost died." She stood there waiting for him to let her come over to him.

"Hmmm," he mumbled, examining the ring on his finger. "What's ...what's that in your hand," he asked, seemingly accepting her answers.

"Oh, this?" she said, holding it up. "This is yours. It's a key, a special key.

"No, the other hand. What are you hiding?" he asked, growing increasingly suspicious.

"Oh, this? she smiled, lighting up her face. "This is yours too."

"Well. What is it then?" He played along, beginning to get her humor a little.

"They call it ..... a pregnancy test."

"Ok ... so let me get this right. You are Casey, my wife. I am Angel, your husband and you are pregnant with our child. Is that correct?"

"And we are in love," she corrected. "Are you sure you don't remember anything?" she asked, desperation growing in her voice.

"Well. I remember a little about my childhood."

"And?"

"I was underwater, sitting on the pool floor lotus position, holding my breath."

"Whatever for?"

"Dad was a Ju-jitsu master. He was teaching me to meditate like him, the way he learned it in Tibet."

"Tibet? What? Wait a minute! Micah Angel Tate, I demand that you tell me right here and now, no jokes. Are you saying you were awake?!!"

"Well ... yes ... and no. I mean at first yes, I tried to meditate as dad had shown me and I began to slow my breathing. I tried to force out the painful throbbing in my head, still, the pain was more than just physical, it was mental as well. I was distraught. So I began to focus on my breathing and ignore the pain as I began to pray. I could hear the beeping of the monitor begin to slow, the soft whirring of the fan in the background and then suddenly I found myself back at Pier 51 where I always used to pray as a child. The familiar beam from the lighthouse on the San Juan Islands stroked across the waters like a sweeping paintbrush. I begged God to take away the pain, to carry us through, to keep you safe. Then everything slowed down like a movie coming to the end of its reel. A quiet calm came over me, encompassing me, comforting my fears. I felt as though I were being carried, wrapped up in his arms and everything was going to be ok. I could let go now. I was assured I could rest now. I could just let go. I was so tired ... I'm not even sure I said 'Amen.'

Psalms 38: 4, 12 – 15

⁴ For my own errors have passed over my head;
Like a heavy load they are too heavy for me.

¹² But those seeking my soul lay out traps,
And those working for a calamity to me
have spoken of adversities,
And deceptions they keep muttering
all day long.

¹³ As for me, like someone deaf, I would not listen;
And like someone speechless, I would not open my mouth.

¹⁴ And I came to be like a man that was not hearing,
And in my mouth there were no counterarguments.

¹⁵ For on you, O Jehovah, I waited;
You yourself proceeded to answer,
O Jehovah my God.

CHAPTER 45

Dear diary,

It has been over a year since that day in the hospital. The Prosecution dropped all charges against him after watching the security video and settled in Civil Court for a modest amount after it was discovered that the State's 'Medical Expert' had no medical license.

The money doesn't matter to me of course, but Micah insisted on super-sizing my wedding ring.

However, what we're most proud of is our new addition. Angelica Tate is crazy smart as she quietly seems to understand what is going on at our religious services …. well …. except for when she's trying to suck the diamond off my ring. The first time it happened Micah leaned over and whispered, "Just like her mother."

When I shot him a look, he continued: "She loves hugs and …"

THE END

ABOUT THE AUTHOR

A TRUE ACCOUNT

My name is Michas Taitano. But sometimes I am called Lefty, The Gingerbread Man, Micah, Hermano and sometimes even AMW. These names are sort of a laundry list of how I became who I am today. But perhaps the name I am most proud of is 'Hermano' and that is because it is Spanish for 'brother,' being as I am a Jehovah's Witness brother serving in a foreign language group.

Now my story has been told many times and I have been interviewed by people of all sorts, sometimes on official business, sometimes just out of curiosity.

Most know something of my past. That I was once a dangerous criminal. That I have lived in or traveled to, at least 9 countries and 30 different cities. In that time I wreaked havoc on the world, eventually I was featured on America's Most Wanted.

But for those that knew me, this was no surprise, as my life had many such dangerous turns. I once counted that I had had a gun to my head at least 3 times, was shot at, was nearly killed by a serial killer, even escaped death after being thrown from a truck at 80 miles per hour. Through all if this I learned nothing.

Until I opened the Bible again.

"What would you say if I told you that I think you are a delusional loose cannon?"

This was the first thing the elder said to me after I'd entered the packed room, surrounded by elders. It was a serious question, as they wished to know who I was. Who I really was. What of the stories on TV? And could I be trusted? When I heard it I almost chuckled. I think I said something like, "Yeah. I've asked myself those same questions a time or two." But it wasn't so long ago that an elder's comment such as that had really caused me to take a new path in life. To examine things from another person's point of view. Specifically one elder by the name of Will Marroquin, famous Witness for his integrity in these parts. (Washington State)

I'll never forget the day. I was in Walla Walla prison. I had just come in and I was told to attack another inmate. Someone I didn't know but who had caused some disturbance to my three cell-mates. They had threatened to do me harm if I did not carry out their orders. But I had a better plan. I would simply kill all three of them. Yes, this was my 'better plan.'

I remember listing off the things I would need before doing it. One, a decent meal. I had been eating the terrible county jail food for too long. Second, watch a Seahawks game. I had missed game after game in county jail. Third, I wanted to go to one service of Jehovah's Witnesses. Then, would be prepared to kill them, and it served them right, I thought, as they had no idea who they were ordering around.

So I ate my meal. Forgettable, save for the coconut pudding. Watched my game. The Seahawks lost, no surprise there. Then, I went to my meeting. Incidentally, I had been walking around with an inmate soldier who was, in effect, just there to make sure I did their bidding without going to the police. Funny thing was, he was willing to follow me everywhere, with the exception of the meeting. So this was the first time Will Marroquin and I had ever laid eyes on each other. So I casually tell him, "Sir, I am dis-fellowshipped. But good news is, I plan to come back. Bad news is, I'm going to kill three men tonight as I have no other choice. It's either kill them, kill a stranger, or be killed, the last being no real option."

He didn't even flinch. He said: "Son, you're a Jehovah's Witness. You can't kill anyone."

"But I'm dis-fellowshipped." I protested. Thinking that I would not be held to account.

"You're a dis-fellowshipped what?" He asked.

"Well. I'm a dis-fellowshipped Jehovah's Witness," I replied.

"So then, you **are** a Jehovah's Witness. So you must obey the Bible."

We talked for a little while as he explained all the principals involved using the Bible. Eventually he asked me to have faith and take his advice. However, his advice was dangerous, if not outright deadly, as I later found out.

Here was the plan:

IN THE BELLY OF THE WHALE

"I want you to take yourself out of the equation," Will continued.

"Out of the equation? How?" I asked, confused and wondering if this old man even knew the seriousness of the situation.

"I want you to ask for a transfer. To a different unit, or perhaps even a different prison."

"But, what good would that do? These men are part of a gang that spans across all the prisons. If word got out, they would simply send someone to get me wherever I happen to be. This is no solution," I argued.

He went on to relate that I had in effect, always followed my own course. And that my lack of faith was directly connected to never having really opened up the door to Jehovah to see what he would do in the event that I did trust him.

It was sobering to consider his advice and the implications thereof. He was basically calling me out on the issue of faith. And in doing so, set forth a course that would be impossible to reverse once started.

I remembered walking out of that room and taking a sharp left to the counselor's office. My inmate guard must've gone back to the cell, as he wasn't waiting outside the door where I had left him.

I went in and told the lady I needed to transfer to another unit. Course, she asked why. I figured I could tell her some of the story without divulging names. So that's what I did. She asked me who, specifically was in danger. Citing that, even if she did remove me from the scene, no doubt another missile would be sent eventually. Missiles are what unknown attackers are called in prison. Well, I remembered the verse I had been shown about doing good to your neighbor and the responsibility of the person who heard of an imminent attack on another. These things in mind, I told her the name.

She left the office and came back a few moments later with the sergeant, who wanted to know, of course, the names of the assailants. This I would not give, as snitching is as good as signing my death warrant in prison. Instead, I simply told him I did not know. This angered him.

Rather than receiving my transfer, I was put in the hole. The hole has many parts and levels. The primary hole is a temporary holding block for the accused. The first stop in the belly of the whale. It is a place where the most violent of men, who, even after arriving in prison for their crimes, still haven't even begun to behave themselves. Much time is spent sending messages to one another via fishing. Fishing is where you'd tie a message onto the end of a string and send it flying down the cellblock.

The other person has a string also, but his is equipped with a hook, with which he catches your line and reels it in. That was for private messages. But most things were not private in the hole. Rather, these men reveled in spinning stories of the most depraved acts and instances of violence one could imagine. Also there were the fights. Pre-arranged by the officers, the doors of two mortal enemies (usually rival gang members) would 'mistakenly' fly open at once forcing the combatants to fight. It was a well- known thing and bets were often taken up long in advance.

The officers guarding the hole were of the worst sort. You see, often these officers would sustain injuries while trying to break up a fight in general population. Or perhaps they had simply been attacked themselves by some angry inmate. Either way, once sustaining a black eye or a swollen lip, they could no longer walk about freely among the general population as the inmates would see the bruise and, like sharks, smell blood in the water. So where to put the officer while he heals? The hole. Likely with the very person who harmed him.

In these places, the law does not exist. The officers read all outgoing mail and will stop any correspondence that would expose the situation. Not to mention that telling anyone outside the walls what really went on in there was one guaranteed way to punch your ticket for an eternal stay in the hole, where they could closely supervise you and ultimately keep all your mail from going out.

This is the place where I was sent and charged with 'conspiracy.' Will's words kept running through my head as it became apparent that this test of faith may just be my end.

The charge was a ploy to get me to talk. But I wouldn't, couldn't, if I hoped to survive. A hit, or an order to kill, made by a gang leader, could be carried out at any time in any prison. The prisons are all connected by word of mouth, traveling with the inmates being transferred between them. There are no secrets. I contemplated that elder's advice as I was processed into the hole.

"Have you any special allergies?"

"No," I muttered.

"Ever thought of committing suicide?"

"Yes," I answered frankly. Little did I realize what that frank answer came with.

I was immediately carried off to the mental ward and stripped naked. Thrown into a rubber walled room with only a small hole in the middle covered by a grate that I assumed was meant for a latrine. So there I stood, naked and cold, asking myself, "How did I get here? Oh yes, Brother Will Marroquin."

About that time there was a knock on the door as the small viewing slot slid open and a small face appeared.

"Inmate Taitano? You have a visitor," came a booming voice.

Guess who? Will Marroquin. Again he showed no alarm finding me naked and in a rubber room.

"Brought you something to read," he said as he shoved the magazines through the small slot after the officer vigorously inspected each page.

"How are you doing," he asked.

The anger boiled up in me like a volcano. "How am I doing? How am I doing? I could've killed those three and have gone to the hole with some respect! But now look at me!" I yelled, moving close to the portal so that he couldn't really look at me fully. (Too much coconut pudding)

"Well, you're alive. And he's alive. I still think you should ask for a transfer to another prison," he reiterated.

"What good would it do? I told you, one prison is the same as another. Only difference is, here I know and recognize my enemies, but there, they will send a missile I do not know. You see what you've gotten me into?"

He didn't seem worried. Instead he said something more about faith that I didn't hear over the roaring from my fear and anger.

Here I had trusted someone other than myself and look where it got me.

A few days later I was told I was going to be transferred back to the hole. But when I heard the cell number I refused. They were going to move me next to the cells where my cellmates were being held, also in the hole. In other words, they were setting up a fight, possibly three on one, or one at a time.

You see, this sergeant was no fool. He knew what was going on in his prison and who wanted whom dead. When I'd entered his office that day he'd had no doubt as to where the orders were originating from. So, he put us all in the hole and pitted us against each other, telling us one at a time that the others would tell sooner or later and that it was best just to come clean now. So we all stayed silent and thus we were all being held until someone told him a story he'd buy. But since no one was talking, a fight would have to do.

This in mind, I refused to leave my rubber room. This really brought out the worst in my attending guard. He called in the extract team.

The extract team is simple. A team of ex-military soldiers who were just dying to rough someone up. They wore full black body armor and carried plastic shields and wooden batons. With the exception of the lead man. He was equipped with an electrified shield that on contact would stop any man dead in his tracks.

I watched as they suited up outside my door. They were so joyful and eager. Each of them peeking in from time to time to get a good look at their prey.

In circumstances like these, your most hardened convicts smear Vaseline on the floor so that the first ones through would slip, giving the advantage to the convict. Others would store up fecal matter in a cup and launch it at the invaders. No doubt this was the reason for my strange toilet. Either way, I had no such plan, but rather prayed, "If you're up there, I just want you to know that what happens next is going to be on you. I could've done things my own way, but instead listened to your representative. Just saying."

About two minutes before the extraction (which I knew because they were loudly counting down) an officer came up to the door and said, "You must have some kind of angel on your side because the lieutenant has over-ruled the extraction and has decided to move you instead to IMU. So will you go peacefully?"

He didn't have to ask me twice, as I put my hands through the portal, feeling the cuffs latch on the other side.

What I did not know then, which I found out all too quickly, was that the hole has many levels of darkness. And my latest relocation was bringing me to Level 3. The worst possible place on earth. The place that houses only the roughest of them all, including Kenneth Bianchi, the notorious killer; Gary Ridgeway, the Green River killer; and Yates, the Spokane serial killer.

By now I had heard that there was a hit out on my name and that my assailants (whomever wanted the job) were ordered to finish me off in the most painful way possible. So there I was in 7 House, listening to the stories of the terror these men wreaked on the weak and helpless. For me, my crimes had come out of my want and desperation, but for these depraved and blood thirsty men, it was sheer sport.

I had no doubt, that if I so much as said one word out loud, the questions would come. With the questions, the inquisition, with the inquisition, the truth. Again, there are no secrets in prison. And with the truth, the attached 'hit order,' and with the order, someone would eventually recognize me and carry that hit order to wherever they went. Making a transfer utterly pointless. Indeed, the only way I was going to have a hope to live past my twenties was to keep my big mouth shut. Say nothing. Anything I said would open up a dialog that would start with the question, "Why are you in here?"

During my first 60 days, I witnessed the cruelty and abuse of the officers. I listened to the blood curdling cries of inmates being beaten in the showers.

I held a toilet soaked T-shirt to my mouth in order to breathe through the smell of mace as one cell after the other was being sprayed down for one reason or the other. Didn't really matter the reason, as the entire unit was on the same ventilation system. Thus, what one of us got, we all got. I would listen to the conversations going back and forth, up and down, as I was on the top tier. I did get mail, thankfully, and so every day I read some material from the Slave. But soon I couldn't read anything at all as my light suddenly went out, leaving me in the dark. I remember that after the fifth day of darkness I entered into a depression so deep that I thought I would never come out. I tried to read my Bible under the sliver of light coming from the tiny window in the early morning light.

"The greatest vanity! Everything is vanity!"
Ecclesiastes 1: 2

I laughed so hard that day (or night, hard to tell) when I read that account. As I had finally been stripped of everything. Money, personal clothing, friends, family, dignity, and now even light. Yet here was a man that had everything and still he was in anguish. The irony did not escape me, neither did the cries of my next door neighbor who cried out daily: "I just wish I knew who the true God was. What is the true religion, the true path?" he would exclaim loudly.

Of course there was no way I was going to answer him. No. And risk my life for him? Remember, silence = life, talky, talky = death, eventually. Besides, he had obviously done something pretty bad to wind up here. So, I had been ignoring him for nearly a month.

Incidentally, each week I would be called into the office to see if I was ready to hand over the names. Each week got the same results, a trip back to my cell. But just that last week it was different. They had told me that one of the others had confessed and that I was being transferred to another prison Monday. But today was Tuesday.

Again I was brought into the office, this time they claimed to have lost all my paperwork and were confused as to who I really was and why I was even there, nevertheless, they assured me, you'll be gone Monday. Another Monday came and went.

By now I had lost my ability to see color from the extended darkness. Yet each night 8 House would start up again: "I wish I could find the true God! I wish I knew the true path!" Yes, it was some kinda Chinese torture for Witnesses. Added to this, each night someone would try to answer his questions of faith, one day it would be Islam, the next the Trinity, the next Buddhism. All of it met with my prayer, "NO JEHOVAH! Absolutely not! I am not going to throw away any hope I have to live to teach this man. Think Jehovah of all the people I could teach in the next prison. That would be hard to do if I'm dead, doncha think? Was it you who cast me into darkness? Have you really commanded that this man should be taught? No! I am not the man for this!"

By now I had entered into what I can only describe as suspended delusion. It was as if the planet had erased me from its memory. My only reprieve had been the steady source of mail coming in. But now even those rivers had dried up, leaving me feeling utterly alone and forgotten. Add to this that I was and always have been a very social person. So keeping my mouth shut for several months was starting to take its toll as I began to vehemently argue with the darkened mirror.

In fact, it had been so long since I'd last spoken out loud that one night someone called out to me. "7 House! 7 House! Are you in there?" "He doesn't speak English!" yelled my neighbor in 8 House. Such was my plight, that even my own language was no longer credited to me.

All that night 8 House cried out in desperation, "Will the true God answer me? Who is the true God?" Maybe he kept it up until morning, I'm not sure. However, I do remember his next words mid-afternoon the next day, "You know what I wish? I wish there existed a book comparing all the world's major religions. In that way I could decide for myself."

I remember looking around my room just to make sure and then finally said: "Ha Jehovah! I do not have the Mankind's Search book! See?" I held out my hands to display the books on my dimly lit bed. By now I should mention that my prayers had become an open format of sorts. Meaning, I no longer opened a prayer nor closed it with "Amen." It was all one long prayer that never ended and so at any time I would just speak as though we had been debating all along on this issue.

The slot to my door opened suddenly. The same slot that my food came through three times a day. But this time it was accompanied with the words, "Taitano. Mail."

I opened the curious brown package, reading its sender: Watchtower.

I nearly fainted when I discovered its contents. Not one, but two, Mankind's Search for God books! One for him and one for me!

"Oh!" I wailed. "Oh, so now you're *Mister Wise Guy*, eh?"

Becoming completely unhinged, as I knew (and still know) for an absolute certainty that I had at no time, ever ordered the books. (To this very day I still theorize as to who might have ordered them.)

"Ok, ok …. I can play this game! So that's what you want, huh? You want me to sacrifice my life to teach this bum? This convict? This one singular person? Although you know what danger it will put me in? You are willing to let me die just to give one singular witness? You turned off my lights? You stalled my transfer? And now you are sabotaging my future for this one man? Ok …. Let's just say I believe it really is YOU. Let's say that it really is YOU doing all of this. In that case, Sir, you have one problem." I picked up a copy of the book and maneuvered over to the door. "You see this?" I asked, while exaggeratedly shoving the book against the invisible seams of the door jam. "Just how do you suppose I get this book out of this air tight door?" I asked incredulously.

Actually, it was a good question. This was the 3rd level IMU. That means no fishing. In fact, these particular cells were built nearly air tight. In fact, I imagined that if I stuck a sock in the toilet and flushed it continually, I would sooner drown that find a breach in their security.

"Ok. So you are God Almighty. And you know full well what happened to me when I was young, just after I was baptized, and why I trust no one. You know all things. Let us speak openly then."

"No more games. I will make you a deal. Right here, right now. If you truly want him to learn the truth, then I swear I will teach him everything I know in the time that I have. I will sacrifice my safety, my future, for him. BUT ..... you have to take this book out of my hands and through this steel door. Amen."

At the exact moment the word "Amen" left my mouth, the door to the unit swung open. No. Not my door. The main door to the unit pod. Enter an officer. I sway back from my cell door as he makes a bee line up the stairs. I am holding my breath in astonishment. But, he does not stop at my door. No, instead, he goes to 8 House and says: "Random strip search! Come out and strip naked!"

I had seen this officer before. Brutal is the only way I'd describe him if it was indeed the same one I remembered. "EXCUSE ME OFFICER!" The words left my mouth almost involuntarily.

The unit dropped into dead silence. Not only did convicts NEVER speak to officers as a given rule, but now it wasn't just anyone speaking. It was 7 House, the mute!

"What the **##!! is your problem 7 House?" The officer bellowed as I braced for the beating sure to come.

"Um, there's a problem." I say with an authority I had been lacking my entire life.

"Yes indeed there is going to be a problem. So what is it?" he growled in the deafening silence, his voice echoing off the walls.

"Yeah, the mail came today," I continued.

"So?"

"So I got this package from New York."

"So what."

"So it isn't mine," I said, wondering if I was actually the one speaking.

"No? Well who's is it?"

"It's his!" I said, pointing to the naked figure on the tier.

He stared at the book for a moment and then opened the slot, yanking it from my grasp. He stood there flipping through the pages. Finally, seemingly satisfied, he marched over to the naked man, slammed it into his chest with force enough to knock the man and the book sprawling into the cell. Finally I heard the cell door slam shut. Silence then ensued as the officer left the unit, the door closing behind him.

"HEY 7 HOUSE!" yelled my neighbor. "Is this a book of all the world's religions?"

"Yes" I said, keeping it simple.

"Hey! Is this printed by Jehovah's Witnesses?"

"Yes."

"MAN, I HAVE BEEN LOOKING FOR THE WINNESSES FOR THREE YEARS!!! Say, what is your name?"

There are stories told about hearing a pin drop. Never could the saying have fit better than at that exact moment.

"MY NAME IS …….. Angelo." (My middle name.)

True to my promise, I spent the entire night educating the entire unit about the true God and his ability to get his will done regardless of the obstacle.

I gave him the address to the Society and assured him that Jehovah was not limited to bars and doors.

That night, I praised Jehovah with my face to the cold concrete until my knees ached. I had barely begun to shut my eyes for sleep that night, when, on a hunch, I went over to the wall and flicked the switch, as I had every day for an unknown period of time. This time though, the lights abruptly lit up the room, blinding me. Smiling, I again tried to get some sleep but was interrupted moments later when I heard it. "Taitano! Turn around and cuff up. Your transfer has come through."

Such was the result of one of the most important interviews of my life, my interview with Will Marroquin. Incidentally, my public prison file reported that even the Warden believed that I had some kind of "Angelic" help. He'd said the strangeness of the events surrounding Taitano's introduction to prison were "Inexplicable"

I was transferred to a lesser security prison and soon thereafter found myself in the room mentioned earlier, surrounded by Christian elders asking questions.

The result of that meeting was my re-instatement as a Jehovah's Witness. But if I had believed that my status as a Christian was going to provide a relief from danger, then that fleeting thought soon vanished after I met my new best friend, James Brett.

Also a baptized Witness, Brett was trouble as I suppose he had been his entire life. Convicted of murder and sentenced to death in the gallows, Brett had very little to look forward to.

Ill-tempered and without respect for human life, Brett becoming a Witness was about as likely to happen as King Manasseh being forgiven.

Funny thing is, Manasseh's conversion was probably easier than Brett's. But Brett had a few helpers, Jehovah and Brother Marroquin.

As it turned out, during the very same time period that Brother Marroquin was assisting me, he was also assisting Brett.

Brett had run out of appeals, denied all avenues to spare his life and was being scheduled for the gallows when he finally qualified for baptism as a Jehovah's Witness.

Then, for no apparent reason, a judge stayed his execution and changed his sentence to life in prison. Brett was baptized a few days later and soon after this he and I met at our new institution and congregation.

However, as I said, Brett was trouble, but this time for a different reason altogether.

I'm not sure what was going on in his mind in those days but he seemed to want to save every unredeemable man in prison. Unredeemable from my point of view but totally savable from his. Perhaps he felt that if he himself could change, then they too could change. A thought process of his that put us in danger time and again.

You see, prison convicts are for the most part and with few exceptions, broken up into groups or sects. Whites, Blacks, Asians, Mexicans and lifer's (life without parole.)

Those exceptions I mentioned are considered the dregs of the human food chain. They include rapists, child molesters, woman beaters and child killers. Being caught even speaking to someone like that could put one's life at great risk, if for no other reason than that these ones were constantly the target of extortion, brutal violence or prison slavery.

Anyone throwing in their lot with these type of people could expect to receive the same treatment. The population would simply conclude that those associating with them had to be just like them.

Well, Brett didn't care about all of that. His first student was in prison for putting a baby in a microwave.

There's a scripture that says that God will not let you be tempted beyond what you can bear. Well, in the following weeks that Brett taught this young man the Bible, I woke up every morning feeling like I was being pushed beyond what I could bear. Everyday Brett was receiving more and more threats from gangs that wanted to harm that new student. I guess they felt that Brett was protecting him. (He was)

Most of the threats were coming from a white gang that seemed to be setting Brett up for an upcoming ambush. All the while I knew that I could not stand by and watch my best friend be killed. And so one night I caught the leader of that gang alone in the TV room. What happened next was not planned and as I approached him I had no idea what I was going to say but what came out was. "Listen buddy, I know who you are and the power you have and we respect you and your group. But we as Jehovah's Witnesses are commanded to preach to the sick which includes those sick in their mind. Brett is my best friend and as such what happens to him happens to me. But we will not stop teaching whomever will listen."

I think the entire conversation lasted only a few seconds – but it felt like I grew gray hairs in bunches in those moments.

As it turned out, Brett's student later rejected the Bible's message and Brett was never attacked. You would think Brett would slow down a bit with the type of students he chose from that point on, but you and I would be wrong.

While we had gained a measure of respect by this point from some gangs, Brett continued to find students that were hated and discarded. His next student, a candidate for a white gang, seemed to accept the Bibles' message. But that message, the Bibles' message, clearly was opposed to joining a gang.

This put Brett and I in the cross-hairs again. While Brett woke up every morning beaming that he had found a lost sheep, I woke up every morning wondering if I should make body armor out of some taped together book covers to protect myself from being stabbed. The first thing to be considered is that I am bigger and stronger than Brett. Thus I would naturally be the first one attacked if they hoped to successfully pull the student away from us.

The second thing to be considered was our former reputations for violence. Anyone attempting an attack would of course take into consideration that attacking two proven killers would require more than a simple punch to the face. Thus the book covers.

The night finally came when Brett and I were going to attempt to escort the student to our religious service, a half mile walk past hundreds of 'could-be-attackers.'

A week prior to this endeavor we had asked a Christian elder what to do if violence was perpetrated against an inmate Witness. His advice was that we should form a 'human shield' around the person targeted 'linking arms' as a barrier.

Sounded like good advice at the time, so off we went, the three of us down the corridor. Brett was in front, the student behind him and I took up the rear.

We headed out single file as masses of inmates pushed their way past us in the crowded corridor.

Then suddenly, the student stopped and went backwards.

"What are you doing?" I asked desperately, adrenaline rushing my words into a slur.

"I've gotta mail these Christmas cards to my family. I know we do not celebrate Christmas but I haven't yet told my family and they wouldn't understand if they didn't hear from me," he replied.

I waited nervously by his side while keeping an eye on the faces in the passing crowd.

I did see one face of a man that passed us quickly who looked as though he were about to do something, but off he went ahead of us. That's when I noticed Brett was gone!

I grabbed the student by his collar and pushed through the crowd trying to find Brett. By the time we found Brett, some fifty yards ahead, traffic had then begun to move in the opposite direction, heading towards us and therefore effectively cutting down my reaction time if indeed one of them was an attacker. Nevertheless, we caught up with Brett safe and sound just a few feet from the chapel doors.

I guess I was relieved to see him safe and so let down my guard. Mistake.

It all happened so fast. One second, the student is standing next to me, the next, he's on the ground being kicked.

The attacker was a small man, the one from the hall, who I had seen as no threat. It simply looked as though we were blocking his path and he was attempting to cut between us.

I barely saw the first punch out of the corner of my eye. I turned on a dime and motioned to attack the attacker. But something stopped me. I could feel it preventing me just as though a strong hand were holding me back from a ledge.

Reasoning entered my brain saying, "It's one on one and the attacker has no weapon. The student is not in mortal danger. But if you attack, the outcome will set up a rivalry between the Jehovah's Witnesses and the other gang. The Witnesses will be viewed as a prison gang from now on and the work of teaching as neutral non-combatants will be over."

Now, I am not saying I heard a voice – or – the heavens opened up. I'm just saying that the reasoning entered my brain as though a computer was being downloaded.

As it turned out, that student too rejected the Bibles' message, but Jehovah's Witnesses as a group, had gained a solid reputation as non-combatant advisors, helping the prison population to see other options to life other that prison gangs.

Our new found reputation was helpful as Brett and I went on to help 10 people to baptism in 10 years. In fact, our reputation as Christian Ministers became so widely known among the population that the inmates would listen to our conversations between the bars to determine if they should avoid us out in the yard or not.

So Brett and I came out with a code. I would ask him, "Are we wearing jeans or sweats?" If he yelled back "jeans!" then that meant we were going to go preach. But if he had said "sweats!" that meant we were just going out for recreation.

It has been 13 years since I first met Brett. We are still Witnesses, we are still best friends and every once in a while I still ask him, "Hey Brett, what are you wearing?"

Taitano, M. currently resides in Washington State.

He is an active member of the Hoquiam Spanish Congregation.

His motto is:
Survive the worst, excel in the best,
But remain loyal during it all.

CHASING CASEY
Is his first published book.

$$\begin{array}{r}117\\31\\\hline 148\end{array}$$

$$150^{.00}$$

$$\begin{array}{r}1072.18\\-150.00\\\hline 922.18\end{array}$$